Missing Dad

1. Wanted

J. Ryan

Matador
9 Priory Business Park,
Wistow Road, Kibworth Beauchamp,
Leicestershire. LE8 0RX
Tel: 0116 279 2299
Email: books@troubador.co.uk
Web: www.troubador.co.uk/matador
Twitter: @matadorbooks

ISBN 978 1784624 743

British Library Cataloguing in Publication Data.
A catalogue record for this book is available from the British Library.

Printed and bound in the UK by TJ International, Padstow, Cornwall
Typeset in 11pt Aldine401 BT by Troubador Publishing Ltd, Leicester, UK

Matador is an imprint of Troubador Publishing Ltd

Wanted

CHAPTER 1

Deep Water

'Do you realize how serious this is, Joe?'

I can't look the cop in the eyes. 'I know it was wrong…'

He shakes his head. 'Joe, you must know that driving underage isn't the half of it. A car that answers the description of yours was at the scene of an accident an hour ago. A lad's been run over.'

Feeling cold, I stare at him. 'I never ran anyone over.'

'You're to come and see Detective Inspector Wellington at the station, ten o'clock Friday. Your parents will need to be there too. Got that?'

'Not my dad…'

'Why not?'

'He went away, a long time ago.'

'I'm sorry to hear that, Joe.' He holds open the door of his patrol car. 'In you get, then.'

Inside, it smells strongly of disinfectant. I clip on the belt and watch as cop number two, who took my car key off me, walks slowly round my Peugeot, looking at the tyres. He reaches inside and switches on the indicators to check them too. Then he gets in, starts the engine, turns on the lights and drives off. With a dull shock, I realize what's going to happen in just fifteen minutes time. My stomach churns and my head starts to thump.

The cop who's driving me pulls away and follows my car. 'What did you think you were doing? Underage, so no insurance, no licence, not even an MOT... do you know how many laws you've broken? Not even counting the hit and run?'

'The hit and run wasn't me! I've never hurt anyone.'

'How many times have you been out in that car?'

'A few...'

'It's young idiots like you that cause the accidents. Is it your car?'

'My grandad gave it me.'

'He's going to be well pleased, isn't he?'

I don't reply. All the rest of the way from Stroud to my house I stare out of the window, wishing that the ground would open and swallow us up. As we turn into the road where I live and slow down outside our house, I can see Mum and Grandad at the gate, looking at my car and talking to the cop. He's handing Mum my car key. Her face is white and she keeps running her hand through her hair. Grandad has his arm round her. They turn as the cop car approaches.

'Dear God, Joe, what were you thinking of?' Tears are glistening on Mum's face.

I feel so sick that I can't speak.

'He has an appointment with Detective Inspector Wellington at Stroud station, ten o'clock Friday morning, Mrs St Aubin. You'll need to come with him. Now, we have to be on our way.'

I stare at the ground as Mum and Grandad watch the cop car drive off. She whispers, 'You know you're in terrible trouble, don't you?'

I nod, shivering in the night breeze. Grandad says, 'Well, standing out here in the cold won't help anything. Let's go inside.'

There's no sign of Jack as we go into the kitchen. Perhaps he's gone to bed and knows nothing about what's happened. Mum sits slowly down at the table and looks at me. 'Joe, if someone had asked me if you would ever do something like this, I would have said absolutely not, that you just weren't the type. Now, I feel as though I hardly know you.'

Grandad pushes his glasses onto the top of his bald head. 'Whatever possessed you, Joe?'

I swallow to try and get my gut back into line. 'I dunno... I s'pose I just really get a buzz out of driving and I thought, like, where's the harm in it?'

'Well, now you know, don't you? A boy's been run over.'

'Mum, you've got to believe me – I NEVER ran anyone over!'

'Then I do believe you, love. But the problem is, will the police?'

Grandad frowns. 'It's serious enough even if they don't charge you with the hit and run.'

'And how much else has been going on that you haven't told us about, Joe?' Mum picks up a pen and twirls it between her fingers. 'I mean, I had no idea you could drive. Who taught you?'

'Steve... in return for me teaching him some French... he's got this French girlfriend.'

'Becks' BROTHER taught you to drive? I don't believe it… how could he do such a thing?'

'We didn't go on the road… just used car parks…'

'And that makes it alright does it?'

'I didn't mean that…'

'God, Joe. This is enough to start me smoking again. How many times have you been out in that car?'

'Not many…'

'Well HOW many? Ten times? Twenty times? I want to know!'

'Less than ten times. Maybe four or five…'

'And where did you go?'

'Small country roads mostly.'

'Where you were less likely to be spotted by the police, I suppose.'

'Something like that…'

'And tonight your luck ran out.'

'Yeah…'

Mum rubs her forehead. 'And are there other things you've been getting up to without telling us?'

'No, I promise.'

'I hope for your sake and ours that we can trust you on that, Joe.' Grandad puts his glasses back in their case. 'Now I think you'd better get to bed, don't you?'

As I stare at the pic of a black Bentley Continental on my bedroom wall, Jack tiptoes in, pyjamas on and blond hair tousled. 'Sorry about all this, mate. I wish I could help.'

'Thanks, bud. I've been a complete idiot.'

'D'you want to come and feed my fish… like, it could take your mind off it?'

'Cheers mate, but nothing could do that right now.'

There's a grey dawn in the sky before I get to sleep, only to dream about flashing blue lights and men in black uniforms.

—m—

The next morning, I'm woken by the phone ringing persistently in the hall below. My eyes feel like they've been rubbed down with sandpaper. Mum answers, and from the tone of her voice I know it's not good news. 'I see. How long for?'

Pulling on my dressing gown, I stumble down the stairs as Mum puts the phone down. 'That was the school. The police have contacted them about last night. You're excluded until further notice, Joe.'

'I'm not sure I could face being there anyway.'

'Joe, it's your education that's suffering now! There are going to be so many consequences of what you've done.'

'I'm crap at school, everyone knows that.'

'Only because you don't try hard enough. All your reports say you have an excellent brain but you just don't use it!'

'Can we not go there again… ?'

Mum taps on her high heels back into the kitchen and grabs her jacket. 'I'll be late for work. You know what, Joe? You are your own worst enemy, vraiment!' The front door bangs behind her. Mum only resorts to her native French when she's really angry.

In the kitchen, Jack's in his uniform, munching sugar puffs. His saxophone case lies next to his school bag. He mumbles, 'It just got worse?'

'It just got worse.'

He pushes the sugar puffs box towards me. 'Want some?'

'No thanks, mate. I'm not hungry.'

When Jack's left for the bus, I go back upstairs to bed, feeling shattered, but I can't sleep. I just lie there and stare at the pic of the black Bentley Continental. Then, I must have nodded off because the next thing I know, the clock says half past four and the front doorbell's ringing as loudly as the phone did earlier. Looking down from the landing window, I can see a cloud of red hair swishing around as its owner tosses her head impatiently. Normally, I'd be over the moon to see that hair, but right now I'm not so sure.

I open the door and Becks' green eyes take me in. 'God, Joe, can't you even be bothered to get dressed? You look such a mess.' She marches into the kitchen and fills the kettle.

I follow her on shuffling feet. 'That's because I'm IN a mess.'

'They're saying all kinds of stupid things in school. You weren't actually driving, were you? You were just in a car with someone else who was underage, surely?'

'I wish it was like that.'

She stares at me, twirling a lock of hair in her fingers. 'So it's true – you were the driver?'

I nod, my face burning under her furious gaze.

'This is all Steve's fault! If he hadn't taught you in those bloody car parks… it was a bad idea from the start!'

'It's all my fault, Becks. No one made me do it.'

'How could you be so STUPID?'

8

'Because stupid is what I am, that's all.'

'And they're saying a kid got run over?'

'Becks, I had nothing to do with that! It's just that they're saying my car fits the description of the one that ran the kid over. Same colour, same make, same model – right down to the mashed exhaust.'

'I don't believe this!'

'You think I'm lying about the hit and run?'

'Of course I don't, you idiot! But it's because you were driving that you're in this huge mess now!' She pours the boiling water into two mugs, adds milk and pushes one of the coffees across to me. 'There must be something we can do to prove your innocence.' Her chair scrapes as she gets up and prowls around the kitchen. 'Is it alright if I grab a cookie – I'm starving.'

'Could you pass me one? I haven't eaten since last night.'

As we crunch custard creams, her eyes flash. 'I know! We'll set up a website – call it Justice for Joe – that's got a good ring. And we'll appeal for witnesses who got a proper look at the hit and runner.'

'D'you think the police would let you? I mean, it's like we're doing their job for them.'

'I'm not going to ask them, am I?'

'I dunno… I'm in enough trouble as it is.'

'We've got to do something, Joe! You can't just sit here and feel sorry for yourself.'

'If only Dad was here… I know he'd think of something.'

Her voice softens. 'You miss him an awful lot, don't you?'

'Don't you miss your mum?'

'I don't miss the rows before she split. And she always preferred Steve to me anyway.'

'That can't be true…'

'It is true.'

'How do you know?'

'She made a habit of telling me. No, I don't miss my mother. What was your dad like?'

'I can hardly remember, it was so long ago that he disappeared. But I know he had a job that was very secret, and you had to be very brave and clever to do it. I'll bet sorting out this hit and run would be a doss for Dad.'

'Can you remember anything else?'

'Only one thing. I'm like, standing on this old bridge in Bristol, way above the river, and he's holding my hand.'

'That must be the Clifton suspension bridge.'

'Your geography was always better than mine, Becks.'

'Stop rubbishing yourself and get some clothes on. We're going for a walk and we're not going to talk about cars at all!'

—⁓—

The walk with Becks and her buying us a Big Mac makes me feel a bit better. But it also brings back the huge ache for Dad. After she's gone home, I go up to my room and search on Google maps for the Clifton suspension bridge. I know I was there with Dad once, all those years ago. If I could just feel close to him again, it might help me get through this…

I wait till two in the morning and the whole house is quiet, then I creep downstairs to the kitchen. Has Mum hidden my car key? I wouldn't blame her if she had. I rummage through drawers and cupboards. I even check out the fridge. Then I see my key, hanging on a hook on the wall with all the other keys, right where it should be. That's when I feel bad. Mum trusts me not to do this. Seeing her reproachful eyes, I feel like something that just crawled out from under a stone. I hesitate for a moment. But Bristol's only half an hour away; I'll be back before anyone wakes up. And I just have to stand on that bridge again, feeling like Dad's near me. I lift the key off the hook.

The garage door squeaks as I swing it open. Terrified that a light will suddenly go on in the house, I slip inside my car with its Pot Noodle and crisps smell, and start the engine. Weaving round Mum's Citroën, I pause at the gate as a cyclist with no lights wobbles past. On the country road that leads to the M5, a fox dashes across right in front of me, his eyes red in the beam of my headlights; I slam on the brakes and just miss him. Then I'm on the motorway, heading south. A sign says it's twenty five miles to Bristol. The suspension bridge shouldn't be too hard to find; according to Google it's a big tourist attraction.

When I'm almost in Bristol, a cop car with flashing blue lights makes my hands go clammy with sweat; but it blasts on past, after some other bad men than me. A grey dawn is just tinting the sky as I drive through streets that are nearly empty, except for the odd dustbin lorry and milk float. Reaching the top of a hill where the road is lined with fancy shops and restaurants, I catch a glimpse of a string of shining pearls hanging against the dark clouds; now I know I'm going in the right direction.

Locking my car, I gaze at this mighty bridge that swoops between the steep, craggy sides of the gorge. At the entrance to the bridge, a Samaritan's sign offers a phone number to anyone who might be planning to look down at that muddy river for the last time. Perched on the railing, a large crow surveys me watchfully as I walk out into the centre of the bridge and stand three hundred feet above the river Avon. The tide is almost out; the lights from the bridge reflect faintly in the dark ribbon of water far below. From the tree-covered sides of the gorge opposite comes the faint trill of birdsong, as the grey tinge on the horizon slowly turns to a smoky pink.

How old was I when I gazed out over this water with Dad? I wonder if he remembers it too. The crow flaps dark wings and floats off the bridge, cruising lazily along the cliff face. A drop of water touches my face. As rain starts to fall lightly, then more heavily, I stare down through all that empty air between me and the river. I haven't got away from anything by coming here. I've just made it worse. And I know what Dad would tell me to do.

A hand suddenly rests on my shoulder, and I turn, going cold all over to see the black uniform behind me. 'You're up early for someone your age, lad. Have you got a home to go to?'

'Er, yeah. I couldn't sleep so I went for a walk.'

'What was it brought you up here? Something on your mind?'

He thinks I was going to jump. It's not about my car at all. 'I have some good memories of being here with my dad, that's all.'

'And where's your dad now?'

'He went away…' Suddenly I can see this cop dragging me off to Social Services. 'But he's coming back soon.'

'So what's the plan?'

'I'm going home.'

'That's the ticket. Mind how you go, alright?'

'Yeah. Thanks.'

I can feel his eyes on my back as I walk right past my car and on down the street. It's now tipping with rain. I keep going for ten minutes until I've put a good distance between me and the cop. Then I double back, hoping frantically that he's not there anymore. The bridge is deserted.

Back in my car, I switch my mobile on and almost instantly it rings. 'Joe?' Becks' voice is urgent. 'Joe, where the hell are you? Your mum's just called me in case you went to my place. She saw your car gone and she sounds ill with worry.'

Staring out of the window, I see Mum's white face against the black clouds. 'Tell her I'm alright… I'm on my way back from Bristol.'

'Bristol! God, Joe…'

'I'm sorry, Becks. I'm sorry about everything.'

CHAPTER 2

Duel

The shining lights of the suspension bridge have just disappeared from my mirror when the engine splutters and dies. I look at the fuel gauge and swear. Only total pillocks run out of juice. Clutching my can, I set off at a run through the pouring rain. A middle-aged woman with a headscarf like the Queen is walking her spaniel. She stops and stares at me like she's going to call the cops to arrest this teenage arsonist. I take a left into a wider street. The Marks and Spencer and the other shops are all closed, but thankfully the Shell garage is open.

As I go in to pay up, a golden Labrador curled up by the counter thumps his tail on the floor. The fat guy at the till must think I look hungry. 'We're doing a meal deal, mate. Another one pound fifty, and you get a bacon and egg triple and a Coke, in with the fuel?'

'I've just eaten, thanks.' At least he's not interested in my age.

The Lab watches with friendly eyes as I head for the door. OK, it's a left out of the garage. Once out of sight, I break into a run again. Down to the end, then right. So why don't I remember this cafe doing Buy A Big Breakfast Get One Free? And where's the M & S?

Rain trickles down my neck as I stare around. Maybe I've gone right past the road where I left my car.

I sprint to the end of the street. On the left, there's a tacky pub doing widescreen footie, and a public toilet next to it. Beyond is a one-way system with a queue of cars in the early morning rush hour. I never came this way. Two men lurch out of the men's. They're about the same age as my grandad and they're looking at my petrol can. The taller man shouts, 'Goin' ter torch a car, chav? Why don'cher, then?'

Running on, I turn a corner into Arlingham Row. Is this it? House after house has a battered For Sale sign outside. Sacks of rubbish loll in the gardens. I'm getting this sick feeling that I had on my first day at my new school, when I couldn't find my way home. I stare at the dark windows.

Then, just as I'm crossing the road, I stop dead. A red Peugeot 206 that looks exactly like mine is parked on the other side. I hurry round the back and check out the exhaust. It's a sports tail pipe, all crunched up, like mine. But I didn't leave my car here. And that computes because this is not my car; the reg plates are different. This machine fits the description of the hit and run car, just like mine did. For the first time in this nightmare, I see a small glimmer of hope. My wet fingers fumble for the buttons on my phone. Click/flash. And another. Click/flash. I'm seeing me showing the photos to Detective Inspector Wellington at ten o'clock. Then, my neck starts to prickle.

She must have crept up behind me so quietly. There's something strange about those eyes, with their cold stare. She's athletic-looking in her black tracksuit; her hair's so short it's almost shaved. 'What the bloody 'ell d'you think you're doin'?'

'I… I didn't mean any harm…'

'Course you didn't, you little shit. Now gimme that sodding phone.'

I turn to run. Her hand shoots out and grabs my arm. 'Oh no you don't!'

She twists until I gasp with pain. I throw a kick at her leg. She loosens her hold, 'Bastard!', and I sprint off like my feet are on fire. Seconds later, an engine revs furiously. Tyres spin in the wet, and there's a thump as her car mounts the pavement. I never thought the hit and runner would be a woman.

My flying feet take me down a narrow alley. At the end, I stop and listen before running on. Street names blur as I dash past. Then, one jumps out at me. Gloucester Close. That's it! I was in Gloucester Road before I took that turn and ran out of fuel. Maybe I'm not that far away from my car.

Gloucester Way. I run for the traffic lights at the end. And at last I'm in Gloucester Road. There's the side street; and there's my car! My twisted arm cramps up as I pour in the fuel. I keep thinking I can hear an engine. As I throw myself into the driving seat, her Peugeot skids round the corner. My engine fires at the second try, and I'm gone.

Her headlights are blazing in my mirror. I don't believe this, it's a car chase now; well, at least the odds are more even. The traffic lights turn to green just as I reach them. I take a right for the motorway; she's still horribly close behind me. Then a double decker stops right in front of me and I get round it, but she can't because of oncoming traffic. All the way to the motorway there's no sign of her. A coach is filling my rear view mirror as I turn onto the M5 slip road so I can't be certain I've lost her. And now I've got another problem: eight litres doesn't look like that on the gauge.

The fuel needle's been jammed on zero for ten minutes when I reach Michael Wood services, but nothing follows me off the motorway. Sweating, I fill up my car, and empty my wallet. With a cheerful smile, the blonde-haired woman at the till says, 'You know, we've got this meal deal going? If you put in…'

'Another one pound fifty… thanks, but I'm eating out.'

The door of the service station closes behind me, and I stare around the forecourt. There's not a car in sight. My phone goes. 'Joe, are you alright? We thought you'd be home ages ago… ?'

'So did I… I've got to go, Becks.'

Back on the M5, two sets of headlights are following about three hundred yards behind me. The clock on the dash says six twenty. I could be home before seven, just when Grandad usually gets up to make a cup of tea for me and Jack. But he and Mum have probably been waiting by the phone most of the night. What am I putting them through?

One of the cars behind me overtakes, and powers away in the fast lane. Now there's only one pair of headlights following. Have I passed the Dursley turn-off? I can't remember. My right arm stabs as I rub my eyes. They feel gritty. It's hard to keep them open.

Suddenly, my rear view mirror blazes with headlights that just keep coming. With a huge BANG, someone drives straight into the rear of my car. My head jerks back and the crash barrier comes towards me so fast I can't brake in time. I bounce off it, fighting to get control. The car's spinning round. Lights flash all over the road, the night sky, and in my head. Then, they go out.

—⚉—

I can smell something hot, like burning rubber. My head throbs. Dimly, I hear the door of my car being wrenched open. She chucks me onto the hard shoulder. 'You just don't get it, do you, shitface?' She lands a kick in my ribs. 'Now gimme the phone, or I'll break your bloody neck.'

My head's banging so hard, I can't think what to do. Suddenly, I hear a voice that I know, whispering in my brain. With my good arm, I reach inside my pocket, and hold the phone towards her. Her hand darts out; not quite quickly enough, as I hurl the phone far out onto the motorway. She sprints after it.

Dragging myself into the driving seat, I glimpse a bright glow of headlights on the horizon. Must be about a mile away. Probably a truck, doing eighty. Maybe, thirty seconds before it arrives? She crouches to pick up my phone.

Not expecting much after that smash, I turn the key in the ignition. The engine roars into life. I shift into first. Then, I can't help glancing back. She's still crouching there, in the middle of the motorway, busily pushing buttons on my phone. She must be looking for

18

the pics of her car. The truck's headlights get bigger and brighter as it thunders towards her. I can see it now. It's a massive thirty tonner. But she's still just pushing those buttons. I'm sure the truck driver can't see her, or he'd be slowing down.

My hand reaches out and hits the horn. She looks up and makes a dash towards me. With a blast from its air horns, the truck howls past the place where she was stood less than a second ago. Her hands tug at my door handle, but the doors are locked. Accelerating back onto the motorway, I look in my mirror. She stands there on the hard shoulder, beside her Peugeot that's the twin of mine. I've thrown her my only chance to prove it wasn't me who did the hit and run. But I'm alive.

Five minutes later, I stare at those headlights again. Chill, idiot. We haven't passed a junction yet. She'll turn off at the next one. The Dursley exit comes and goes, and she's still there, getting closer. The phone's not enough, is it? She wants to punish me, for daring to kick her leg, when she wanted to break my arm. For making her run after my mobile, like a dog after a bone. That voice in my head whispers to me again.

I start to veer from side to side, as though I'm losing control. Then I slow down, like my engine's about to blow up. She's still getting closer. But this time, if she tries it again, I'm ready to snap down a gear and get away from her. Now I know she'll follow me wherever I go. And I know where I'm taking her; it's not far now. My eyes never leave the mirror.

Junction 13. I indicate left; the car behind does the same. I don't know how long it takes to reach Stroud;

my head's drumming so hard I've lost all track of time. I vaguely remember turning up Magistrates Road. She's still right in my boot, so out of her brain, she hasn't noticed.

I turn into the steep down-slope of the police station carpark and slam on the brakes. Hit the horn. And keep hitting it, bracing my arms against the steering wheel. There's another huge bang as she shunts my Peugeot right into the back of a really fancy Vauxhall chase car.

A twirling splinter of bumper flying up into the dark is the last thing I see. The last thing I hear comes from a long way off. Detective Inspector Wellington says, 'A bit early for your appointment, aren't you, Joe?'

CHAPTER 3

Shadow on the Wall

My neck's itching, but I can't get at it. Slowly, I open my eyes and stare at a white ceiling. My head thumps. I move my right arm cautiously; it feels like it's been mauled by a lion.

'How are you doing, Joe? Don't move your neck; it needs to rest.' The nurse's voice is soft and friendly as she smiles anxiously.

'I'm… good.'

'You've had a nasty case of concussion, Joe. Your family have visited several times, and your sister came in again yesterday, but you weren't quite with it, I'm afraid. I'm sure they'll be in again today.'

I wonder how a sister was born to us while I was away. I don't ask if she had red hair and green eyes. 'That's family for you. Never there at the right time.' I'd kill for a Big Mac or cheesy chips. 'Can I have something to eat?'

'I'll get you some ice cream.'

Just after I've had my third bowlful, DI Wellington comes in and sits down next to me. He looks a bit like Grandad, with his balding head and bushy eyebrows. 'How's it going, Joe? You up for a chat?'

'I'm up for it.' I tell him everything, right up to the Car Wars finale in his back yard. 'That woman… she had my phone…'

'We've found your phone, Joe. And the photos.'

'Of her car? She didn't delete them?'

'Her lookalike Peugeot was on your phone, in glorious technicolour. We'll soon be able to identify where it was parked when you took the photos.'

'But… was it her? Was she the hit and runner?'

'We've traced her movements from her phone. We know where she was when the hit and run happened. Right on the scene.'

'So… it's official? It wasn't me?'

'It wasn't you, Joe. Fortunately, the lad who was hit is making a good recovery – which doesn't, of course, make things any less serious for our culprit.' He gets up. 'I'll be in again tomorrow. We'll know more about her by then. And there's certain to be more questions I have to ask you.'

He's gone, just when I have so many more questions to ask him. Then the room explodes as my noisy family fills it up. My new sister stuffs a brown paper bag into the cupboard beside my bed. 'Grapes, Joe. Vitamins for the invalid.'

I can see it's a box of chocs, so I forgive her slightly sarcastic tone. 'Thanks, Becks. You always know what's best for me.'

Jack grins, in his usual annoying way. 'Love the neck gear, Joe. Looks, well…'

'You've had your hair cut, then? Looks a bit less girly.'

He runs a hand proudly over the commando-like crew cut. 'It got me three detentions, so it has to be well cool.'

'How's your poor neck, love?' Mum puts her small hand on my forehead; it feels like a butterfly.

Grandad pushes his thick-rimmed glasses up onto his bald head, then takes them off and gives them a polish with the corner of his jacket.

I swallow. 'I'm sorry, I really am.'

Mum's brown eyes glisten while she smiles. 'The main thing is, you're safe, love. And now the police know you didn't do it. We never ever believed you did.'

Grandad clears his throat and puts his glasses back on. 'There's still the driving underage, Joe. It's a serious business. You'll have to face up.'

'I know it was wrong.'

He gives my arm a gentle pat, like it could fall off any time. 'We'll be with you, Joe. See it through together.'

Mum plants a light kiss on my cheek. 'Now, we don't want to tire you, love…'

Jack sticks his head back round the door before he goes. 'Don't bin the scarf, Joe. I'll write the first line of my new song on it. It'll sell for millions when I'm famous.'

They must think I want to talk to Becks. But I'm not at all sure about that. Because Becks is stood there, hands on hips, and her eyebrows are joined up. 'If you'd just come home when I said, you wouldn't be here now, you idiot.'

'I didn't look for this, Becks, honest. It found me, when I found my car.'

'Your car – again! How many more times is your driving going to get you into trouble, Joe? God, I sound like your Mum, except she…'

'Didn't have a go at me. Nor Grandad. But someone has to, I s'pose.'

'They're too relieved to give you a good kicking! It's what you deserve, you know that, don't you?'

'Sorry.'

'Don't patronize me, Joe, or I'll pull that neck brace off, really quickly!'

Slowly, I fish inside the cupboard for the brown paper bag and hold out the box of Heroes. 'Simon Cowell wouldn't dare patronize you, Becks.'

She tips the whole lot out onto the bed, sits down and grabs all the solid Dairy Milks. Unwraps two and munches on them, handing me a toffee. 'What's the food like in here?'

'It was good till I cleaned them out of ice cream.'

She looks around the room. 'No TV. How are you coping without Top Gear?'

Cue for a slightly pathetic grin. 'The nurses make up for it, Becks. White is definitely the new black.'

She scoops up the rest of the Heroes and chucks them straight at me. Then she leans forwards and gives me a hug. Her hair tumbles in long curls all over my face, and tickles my nose. Well worth the shooting pains in my neck.

—᠅—

The next day, Mum comes in alone. She still looks pale, but she smiles brightly as she sits on the chair next to me. 'They said that you'll be home in a couple of days.'

'Mum… is it alright if I ask you a question about Dad?'

Her face tenses. 'What kind of question, love?'

'Did he take me to Bristol once? To the suspension bridge, just him and me?'

Her brown eyes look beyond the room we're in. 'Yes, I remember. He was home on leave. He said a colleague of his had sailed over in his yacht from Marseille and was going to be moored for a few days in Bristol Marina. They planned to meet up, and he thought you'd enjoy coming along. You were probably watching the yacht from the bridge as she went up the river to the harbour.'

'How old was I?'

'Oh… let's see… maybe four?'

'Mum, do you know where Dad is now? If he's alive?'

She takes my hand. 'It would have been cruel to make you hope that he would come back one day. I wondered if I should tell you he was dead… but that would have been wrong too, because I didn't know. I still don't.'

'Why don't you know, Mum?'

'After he disappeared, I was told that even talking about your father could put him in greater danger… and could be harmful to us as well.'

'What kind of danger? I mean, you told us once that his job was very secret, and he had to be very brave and clever… Was he some kind of warrior or spy?'

Mum looks at me long and hard. 'All your father could tell me was that he was a commander in an elite group working against some very powerful criminals. Every day, I have to live with the thought that they might have captured or even killed him. And now, I'm afraid you share that burden too, Joe.' She gets up and goes to the window.

'Aren't they trying to rescue him? I mean, they can't just abandon him…'

She shakes her head. 'I'm sure they'll never give up on your dad. But that's not the kind of information they can share with us.'

'Is that why we moved?'

'I was advised to, yes, just in case.'

'And is that why our last name is St Aubin now, and not Grayling?'

'They felt it would be wise for us to use my maiden name rather than your father's name.' She turns from the window and her face is drawn. 'I'm so sorry, Joe, but you and Jack were both far too young to understand. Even now... I wish there was a way of protecting you.'

'How can you bear to live like this, Mum?'

'What else can we do?'

I think for a bit. 'Mum, there is something.'

She winces, like I'm going to ask her another impossible question.

'I can't remember what Dad looks like. Have you got just one pic I could have? Please?'

She nods, biting her lip. 'I've got them locked away.'

'I'm sorry, Mum. About the driving.'

Her voice has a weary sadness. 'So am I, Joe. If I'd told you sooner about your dad, things might have been different.' She catches me in a hug that's surprisingly strong for her tiny build. And for a few brief moments, I feel a bit less like a shipwreck in a Force Nine going on Hurricane.

—☁—

Mum comes again in the afternoon, and her eyes look like she's been crying as she takes an envelope from her handbag. 'It must have been taken more than ten years ago. One of his colleagues is in the picture... I don't know who it is.'

'Do you have any kind of hunch what's happened to him, Mum?'

Her eyes are faraway. 'Your father was always half in love with danger. It seemed to make him feel alive, in a way that the ordinary things of our existence did not. But now, if he's in severe danger, the last thing he would ever do is bring it home with him.' She kisses my forehead. 'Now I'd better go – have to get tea.'

As soon as she's gone, I rip open the envelope. And find myself gazing into blue eyes full of laughter. It's like Dad's been caught cracking a joke with a mate; maybe the man in the background, who has grey eyes, dark hair and a smile that's not quite a smile. Dad's wearing a white top, his skin is tanned and his smile is open and trusting. Jack and I have his pale blond hair colour.

Tears sting my eyes, and I understand why there aren't photos of Dad all over the house. Even if it was safe to show his pictures, how could any of us bear to be reminded, day after day? I feel angry. Cheated. Did he chuck me up in the air, like celebrity dads do in OK Magazine? How much of us can he remember?

But at least now I can look at him and feel comforted that it really was just him and me on that old bridge over the river. And I know it was his voice in my head that got me away from that horrible woman.

—ᴍ—

Around eleven in the evening, Wonder Nurse comes in with a smile on her face, and a tray. 'This should help you to get a good night, Joe.' I've been prescribed burger and chips. Every insomniac should be on this.

I'm in a comfortable doze now, half-listening to the rattle of trolleys being pushed past the door, the clink of cups and glasses, and nurses talking quietly as they take tea and medicine around. Then it's all quiet, apart from a faint humming. Maybe it's a generator; it never quite goes away.

Something's changed. The light… there's more of it in my room than there was just now. My eyes half open, I blink, and everything's a blur. But there is definitely more light. Little by little, without a sound, the door's opening. Perhaps it's Wonder Nurse with some more ice cream. But I'm sure it isn't. We've had all the food we're going to get till tomorrow. And the door's still opening.

An enormous shadow slides slowly onto on the wall. Then a bulky figure in a black coat glides in so quietly, I can't hear any footsteps. Now, it's just standing there at the end of my bed.

I lie so still, I think I might forget to breathe. I can hear my heart crashing against my ribs, so loudly that I'm sure this stranger can hear it too. I close my eyes again, because I have the feeling that the stranger can see if they're open. I can hear breathing, and it's not me, I don't dare. I can smell something, too. Can't work out what it is, my brain's paralysed.

Then, I can't hear the breathing anymore. I open my eyes, and the room's empty. The door's closed again. All that night, I watch the slits of light around my door. It's the longest night of my life.

When bacon and eggs arrive for breakfast, I just stare at the plate. DI Wellington turns up a few minutes later. 'The food's not that bad, is it, Joe?'

'I have to get out of here.'

He frowns as I tell him about my uninvited guest. Then he goes to the door and closes it, muttering under his breath, 'They didn't waste any time, then.'

'What d'you mean? Who's 'they'?'

He takes the two-way radio from his belt and hits a button. 'Dave? When you're ready, son.'

'Are you saying you know who that dude was?'

He walks over to the window and parts the blinds. 'Not yet. But we know enough now to take a few sensible precautions.'

'Have you found out about her?'

He looks out of the window. 'Leah Wilks. Kicked off her PE instructor's college course for assaulting another student. Got in with the wrong types, and went from bad to worse. She's known for being unpredictably violent. She's now a driver for a group of people in Bristol who are not the types you'd want to party with, Joe. She was doing a delivery for them in Stroud, that night.'

'It's drugs, isn't it?'

DI Wellington turns away from the window to look at me. 'What makes you think… ?

'I had these mates who asked me to drive them places sometimes. I know I shouldn't have. And I always wondered if they had some stuff on them, but I never asked.'

He shakes his head, his eyes sombre beneath those bushy eyebrows. 'Joe, none of this is in any way your fault. Get that into your head. Plus, the local dealers who are known to us are bit players compared to the people you've had a brush with.'

'So… who are they?'

'They're part of something far bigger, we know that much. Now listen, Joe. Wilks will be out on bail tomorrow. We've questioned her, but she won't talk. Too scared of her employers, probably. However, she's attracted so much police attention that she'll be no more use now to whoever's paying her. '

'Is that bad news for her?'

DI Wellington's voice is grave now. 'It could be bad news for you, Joe. Organisations like this never forget. They're a kind of Mafia. They won't be at all happy about their driver being involved in an investigation that could lead the police to them.' His glance goes briefly towards the door, then back to me. 'They could be looking for revenge, Joe. We're taking that possibility seriously. You need to take it seriously, too.'

'D'you mean that dude… last night… ?'

Quick, heavy footsteps in the corridor, the door swings open and Robocop powers into the room. I stare at this Man in Black who's towering over me. And at the 9mm revolver in his belt. DIW says, 'Joe, meet Dave.'

A grip that could crush solid rock like cornflakes imprisons my hand. Dave grins, 'How're you doing, mate?'

'Dave will make sure that you have no more unwanted visitors while you're in here, Joe.' DIW gives me his card. 'And once you're out on your own, call me if you're worried about anything. Anytime.'

Dave grins at me again, as DIW leaves. 'And you will tell me if my jokes are a pain in the neck, won't you, Joe?'

That night, I keep hearing Mum's voice in my dreams, all jumbled up with DI Wellington's...'working against some very powerful criminals... organisations like this never forget...'. But it's not like I feel scared this time. I'm tingling all over at the idea that somewhere in all this could be a clue that might lead me to Dad.

—m—

'Your poor old car.' Becks peers in through the open window, and wrinkles her nose. 'Smells even worse than before.'

'They've probably disinfected it. Takes a pretty good immune system to go over my car and look for clues.'

'What clues?'

'Well, you know. Her DNA?'

She withdraws sharply. 'Eeugh!'

It's creepy to see my car right next to that woman's again. The police garage is littered with bashed up cars and bits of car. On the other side of mine, there's a Merc SLK with no bonnet, and just a huge hole with dangling hoses and wires where the engine was. Next to her Peugeot, a red Ferrari looks like it's had a too-close encounter with a tank. Behind us, there's a double decker that must have thought it was a single decker, just before it tried to go under a low bridge that had no such idea.

DIW has disappeared into an office and now he emerges holding a carrier bag. 'You can have these back now, Joe. We didn't think you'd want the empty crisp packets, though.'

In the bag are my CDs and an old hoodie that was in the boot. 'Thanks.'

'How's the neck?'

'It's coming good.' I finger the brace. Wonder Nurse and Dave both signed it before I left the hospital yesterday. Dave wrote, 'Chin up, Joe!' Very funny.

'Have you seen anything more of your visitor, Joe? Any kind of hint that he's still around?'

'No. It was good having Dave outside my door. I got some sleep after that.'

DIW's look takes us both in as he says, 'You could still hear from these people again, Joe. When the Wilks case comes up, you'll be called to testify against her as a witness for the prosecution. There could be some of her people in court. And they'll be watching you.'

'And you'll be there, watching them watching me?'

Becks grabs my wrist behind my back and twists it so hard I swallow a yelp. At least it's my left arm.

DIW's not joking at all. 'Yes, Joe, we'll be there, watching everyone. But we don't know yet what they're part of. We can only wait for them to make their next move.'

As Becks and I walk down to the bus station, she takes my hand lightly, no hint of GBH this time. 'So, what's happening in the Joe department now?'

'I've got a temp handling shipping orders in this place that makes ball bearings, or something. Dave gave me a hand ringing round, while I was stuck in the hospital.'

She frowns. 'But you're not excluded now that they've caught that woman. And school's not over for two more weeks.'

'I've got a note from the hospital. And the teachers won't miss me, Becks. I'm not exactly one of their great A star hopes.'

'I'll miss you, Joe. I'll call you tomorrow night. Take care.' She squeezes my hand, and the warmth of hers comes as a shock. I hadn't realized how cold I was.

CHAPTER 4

A Message from the Underworld

'Coffee, Joe?' Lenny puts the plastic cup beside my keyboard, with some sugar packets, as I type the columns of figures into the spreadsheet.

'Thanks, bud.' I break my Mars and hand half over. He bites into the chocolate, and sits down with his coffee.

Lenny could be a boxer: shaved head, broken nose and a scar below his right eye. He's black but he was born in London, has a big brother, Jamie. Lenny does packing, while I slave over a nervous computer that keeps crashing. They gave me a desk job because they said I had a disability, so I couldn't work in the warehouse. I wondered what on earth they meant before I realized it must be this neck brace that I can't wait to get rid of.

'Plannin' to be 'ere for a while, Joe?'

'I haven't really thought about it that much. I need the dosh, but I wouldn't mind something a bit more, like, vibrant?'

'Nightclub? Worked in one, once. Doorman.'

'Is that how you got the scar, Lenny? Chucking people out?'

'Nah. 'Elping Jamie. Accident.'

'Does Jamie work here too?'

'Nah.'

I type in some more figures while Lenny munches on his Mars. Then he says, 'Inside. Fitted up.' He chucks his empty coffee cup in the bin. 'Seen the new Bond, Joe?'

We pick the new cinema in the middle of Stroud as it's less far to go than Gloucester and they do better popcorn. As Lenny and I go in, a dark haired dude is stood at the door but he's no doorman. I can feel his eyes on me and it makes my skin crawl. Then Lenny grabs my arm and propels me up to the ticket desk. 'Keep away, Joe.'

'Why?'

'He 'elped fit up Jamie.'

I don't think any more of it until we leave the cinema and start walking up the road for a Big Mac. The street's well-lit and yet I have an uneasy feeling that we're being watched. Lenny takes quick glances behind from time to time. We round a corner to the street where the McDonald's is and suddenly there they are: three big blokes in hoodies who look about as friendly as a Pit Bull that's missed its dinner. They stand completely still, barring our way. The middle one looks like the dude who was standing at the door of the cinema earlier. He has a swaggering grin on what we can see of his face.

'You ain't grown up enough to be out this late, are yer?'

Lenny says just one word, very quietly, 'Move.'

'Oh, I don' think so. Not until this scum's been punished for arse licking men in suits.'

Thug on the left goes for Lenny and the one on the right lunges towards me. Next thing I know, I'm in a headlock that makes Wilks' grip feel like a polite handshake. Through a blur I see Lenny kick his thug in the groin. As he goes down roaring in agony, Lenny grabs Thug in the Middle by the neck and bangs his head so hard on the wall I can hear the crack. I don't see the head make contact because I'm staring at a knife that's right in front of my eyes. My thug says to Lenny, 'You move, he gets it.'

Lenny just nods at the inert bodies on the pavement. 'Two 'gainst one not good.'

The knife wavers as Thug on the Right considers these odds, and Lenny lands a massive karate chop on his shoulder. The knife flies out of his hand and he howls with pain as he disappears up the road. Scrambling to their feet, his mates look at Lenny with undisguised fear and back away, breaking into a run.

'The Big Macs are on me, Lenny.' Sat at a table with our Cokes and burgers, I rub my neck while Lenny swigs his Coke as though this rather too-close encounter never happened. 'Where did you learn to fight like that?'

'Jamie. Why they after you, Joe?'

'There was a hit and run in Stroud a week or so ago. I was the prime suspect because my car fitted the description of the one at the scene. Then, quite by accident, I happened upon the real hit and runner – her car was just like mine. I handed her to the police. They told me she was working for a drugs gang.'

'You betta keep your eyes open, Joe.'

'You mean, they'll be back?'

He nods, and I remember DI Wellington's sombre warning. On the way home that night, I keep finding myself looking behind me, and I avoid taking shortcuts down narrow alleys. At the bus stop, I look at the other passengers, but there are no hoodies among them, just a couple of mums with buggies and an old guy in a crumpled mac who keeps whistling tunelessly. But as I get off the bus, a guy in jeans and a casual jacket follows. Flicking a glance at him over my shoulder, I glimpse dark, crew cut hair and an olive complexion. I speed up to get ahead of him, but he speeds up too, always staying about twenty feet behind me. The road is empty except for the two of us. We're nearly at my house. But I don't want him to find out where I live. So I walk right past the gate and on down the road.

The nearest shop is the Co-op, where we get the bus to school. My heart's thumping as I hear the sound of those footsteps behind me. I'm tempted to break into a run, but he could be faster. By the time I reach the Co-op I'm pouring with sweat. I walk quickly inside and he goes straight past. But that could be a trick. For a good five minutes, I wander up and down the aisles, getting some funny looks from the sales assistants.

'Are you trying to find something?' The skinny teenage girl stacking shelves frowns slightly as she asks.

'Er, yeah… have you got any mint Aero?'

She gives me a pitying look. 'It's next to the checkout, where it always is.'

After I've bought the Aero, I can't start roaming around the shop again, so I go to the door and peer carefully right and left. There's no sign of him. But I still run all the way home.

'You alright, bud?' Jack looks out from his room as I puff and pant up the stairs.

'Just thought I'd try and get myself back into training. This desk job's not good for my blood pressure.'

—◊—

Next morning, I'm back at the computer, typing in figures, my mind still hearing those feet. From out of nowhere, a coffee cup appears, and I jump a mile high.

'You alright, Joe?'

'Sorry, Lenny. I just thought I was being followed last night. And I'm wondering, is it always going to be like this?'

'They scare you like that, they've won. That what you wan'?'

'No, you're right, Lenny. I'm not going to let them take over my life.'

Lenny and me start to hang out some places together. We go to gigs, do some more films. We talk about how we could both get a better job than this, one day. Get rich, holiday in Antigua, buy a whole collection of exotic cars. Lenny fancies a Lambo. We often sit in my room, surfing the net. Then, one evening, we see it. It's a new website, linked to the job agencies. It's looking for drivers. And one of the ads hits me straight between the eyes.

The gold Bentley Continental has lines so powerful it looks like it's doing a thousand miles an hour when it's just stood there. Holding the driver's door open, like he's just about to get in and drive the Le Mans 24-hour, is a chauffeur in a black uniform and black peaked cap. He looks about my age. I hardly notice the blonde girl in the background, with sleek hair, glittering evening dress and impossibly high heels. The ad goes:

L'Étoile Fine Wines

Chauffeur required for Chief Executive of exclusive French fine wines company based in Bristol. Advanced driving skills essential. The successful candidate must also be willing to work flexible hours

It says to email the Personal Assistant of the Chief Executive of L'Étoile Fine Wines with your CV and a letter. She's called Madame de L'Étang.

'Take in that car, Lenny!'

But he shakes his head. 'Not this one, Joe.'

And half of my mind agrees with Lenny, telling me just what Becks would: 'You complete idiot! After all the trouble driving that car got you into, all the rules you broke...' And I can hear my mum, and somewhere a lot further off, my dad.

But the other half of my mind can only see that amazing Bentley, and it's yelling at me, 'This is your big chance, maybe your only chance, to prove you're not a loser!'

Lenny doesn't know I'm not old enough to drive legally, but he still shakes his head. 'Don' go there, Joe.'

'What's the problem, Lenny? I bet the pay's amazing.'

'You don' wanna work for these people, Joe. B'lieve me, you don'.'

'But I do want to work for them! Look, Lenny, driving's the only thing I can do well. Don't you see? If I get this job, it could be the best thing that's ever happened to me!'

He shakes his head again, and the scar below his eye is red now. 'Or could be the worst thing, Joe.'

'But why, Lenny? We both want to get out of this place, don't we?'

'Sure. But not there, Joe.'

I really don't want to embarrass him, because I know he can't drive. 'OK, let's forget it.' We look at some other websites then he dosses down in my room, and we go off to work the next day as usual.

That day, I don't ask Lenny home to surf job websites. 'I'm shattered, need an early night.' I'm up until gone midnight, making my CV look really good, and putting together a letter that makes me come across like a dude Lewis Hamilton loves to hate.

Next day, as I shut down the computer, I can't wait to get back and look at my email. Lenny says, 'Sub Rooms for the gig?'

'Sorry, mate, I promised to help Mum clean up my room.'

'S'cool. See you t'morrow, Joe.'

I check my email. There it is. I'm invited for a job interview as chauffeur for the Chief Executive of L'Étoile Fine Wines. It's for a week today. Madame de L'Étang doesn't ask for references or anything, not like the other jobs I've had where I even had to bring my passport to prove I was me. Her email says: 'The interview will take from 11.00am until 4.00pm and it will involve some driving. I attach a location map for your guidance.'

The next morning, I miss my break and go outside to phone the job agency and tell them that I can't be at work that day. Then I see Lenny right behind me, with a coffee for me. 'Day off, Joe?'

'I have to take my grandad for a doctor's appointment.' The lie comes to me so easily it worries me a bit. This is the third lie I've told Lenny. Actually, it's the fourth, if I count not telling him I was going to apply for the job. I hate lying, but he'd be really bothered if he knew.

In the evening, Mum's loading the dishwasher. I give her a hand, trying to prop up glasses the way she can and I can't. 'I've got a job interview tomorrow, Mum.'

She straightens up, wiping a smear of tomato sauce off her hand with the dishcloth, and I can hear Worried in her voice. 'That's great, love. Who's it with?'

'It's this fine wines company, in Bristol.'

She bends again to jam a bowl into the rack. 'Bit of a commute, then? What's the job?' She's wearing a belt with her jeans. She's thinner. It's me, isn't it?

'Same sort of thing that I'm doing now, but the pay's better.'

I swallow, as more lies trip off my tongue. To my mum, this time. She smiles, and I can see the shadows beneath her eyes. 'Good luck, love. But you must make a big effort to catch up on your school work when term starts.'

'Is it alright if I borrow one of Dad's suits? I need to look really smart…'

She hesitates only for a second, but I feel bad, like I'm trying to step into Dad's shoes, as if anyone ever could. 'Yes… yes, of course you can.'

In the lounge, Grandad's sat in his usual armchair, his bald head nodding gently. The TV babbles away with the news. A sailing magazine's sliding off his lap and his glasses are about to follow. He looks so peaceful that I just stand in the doorway for a few seconds. Then, I think about how tomorrow is going to be the most important day of my life. I go quietly over to him. 'Can I look in Dad's wardrobe for a suit, Grandad? Got a job interview tomorrow.'

He looks up, blinking. 'Course you can… course…' His head nods forwards again, and his glasses topple to the floor. I put them gently back in his lap. Then I tiptoe out of the lounge and go upstairs.

Dad's clothes are kept in the wardrobe in Grandad's bedroom because his room is bigger than Mum's and has a bathroom next to it. Grandad came to stay a few months after the time when Dad went away and didn't come back, and we had to move house and change our name. I can hardly remember anything about our old house now, except that it was quite a lot bigger than the semi where we live now.

I slip into Grandad's room and open the wardrobe. It's an old-fashioned wooden one with brass handles on the doors and on the drawers beneath. The door squeaks quietly as I swing it open. A tangy, fresh smell hits me – not the musty oldness that I expected. And suddenly

I'm back on that bridge in Bristol, but this time I'm with Dad and it's bright day.

The tide is flooding in; it's so high that it's almost at the top of the banks, completely covering all the mud. I must be very small in this memory because I have to look down at the river from beneath the top rail of the bridge. One of Dad's hands is holding mine and the other is waving at the graceful, single-masted white yacht that's motoring smoothly up the river towards us. A man is at the wheel of the yacht and he's waving back to Dad, but I can't make out his face all those hundreds of feet below. Then my attention is caught by the way the sun makes the golden hairs on Dad's arm sparkle, and I look away from the yachtsman.

As quickly as it's come, the image goes; but the scent remains. I suppose it's Dad's aftershave. And that memory was the one Mum was talking about in the hospital. I wonder if the yachtsman is the other man in the photo.

My hands reach out and touch the smooth fabrics of the suits; Dad has some classy clothes. Checking out the sizes, I'm about the same as him now. Carefully, I lift out a dark grey Balmain and team it with a white shirt and light grey tie. That tangy smell wafts across my nose again as I take out the shirt. It's spotless, like it's been washed and ironed quite recently. Does Mum keep Dad's clothes fresh for him, ready for him to walk in the door as though he's never been away? Is that how adults keep their memories and hopes alive?

Wondering if Grandad has any photos of Dad, I take a quick glance around. There's just one black and white pic which I guess is him and Gran on their wedding day, with her in a long lacy veil and Grandad looking about eighteen. Suddenly, all this staring into the past is too much. Tomorrow is where my future begins, and no matter what it takes I'm going to find my dad.

As I head into my room, there's a shout from across the landing. 'Hey, Joe, come and see what my angel fish are doing – it's amazing!' Dad's clothes draped over my arm, I pick my way carefully across Jack's saxophone, keyboard, drum kit and guitar, and stare into the tank. 'They look great... just, having a meal?'

The lights from the tank illuminate Jack's excited face, as the disc-shaped, rainbow-coloured little fish with their trailing fins glide slowly around a plant leaf, where a cluster of tiny eggs lies beneath a thin, glistening film. 'The male is eating the eggs the female laid.'

'Right. Is that good?'

'Not for the eggs, I s'pose. And they both looked so proud of them yesterday. But the female just doesn't seem to mind, does she? You'd think she'd go mental.'

'She looks cool. Why is that?'

Jack sits down on his bed, and plays a few Pink Floyd chords on the keyboard. 'That's fish for you. They just have different priorities. Easier to understand than teachers.' He looks at Dad's clothes. 'Got an interview?'

'This fine wines company in Bristol.'

'Go for it, bud.' Jack's fingers fly across the keys to give me a full orchestra fanfare as I duck into my room.

Mum shouts from below, 'Hey, you two! Time you were both in bed!' But I have to practise for tomorrow as I've never worn a suit in my life. The shirt and tie go on easily because I do those every day for school. I was worried that the jacket and trousers would be too big but they fit perfectly. Should I button the jacket? I reach to the back of my drawer and take out Dad's photo. 'What am I supposed to do, Dad?' His blue eyes look at me, amused.

'It looks better unbuttoned.' Mum has come in silently behind me. Her eyes are shining and she whispers, 'Dear God, Joe, you look so like your father it's terrifying.'

I give her a hug. 'Don't be terrified, Mum.' And for once I shut my big mouth. I don't tell her about my small shred of hope and my huge ambition, because it could be the cruellest thing anyone could do to her.

CHAPTER 5

Precious

I catch the nine o'clock bus from Gloucester to Bristol and sit fiddling with my tie. I never thought I'd look good in one of my dad's suits. I've binned the neck brace – doesn't go with Balmain. Nervously I check through my pockets to make sure I still have Madame's email. And that's when my fingers encounter something I didn't put there. Taking it out, I stare at this small plastic disc. It looks like mother of pearl the way it's textured and the colours shift in the light. On the orange circle in the centre there's the number 10. And around the number are the words 'SOCIÉTÉ DES BAINS DE MER MONACO'. Bains de mer? Sea baths? Is this a kind of swimming club in Monaco? Looking more closely I can see the number '18663' bevelled into the outer ring of the plastic.

Completely baffled, I slip the little disc back into Dad's pocket and concentrate on getting from the bus station to the docks in twenty minutes. The last thing I want is to arrive in a lather of sweat.

Finding the place is no problem. Right in the centre of Bristol, by the docks, and it's so cool – it's sub-zero. A tower of blue glass rises into the sky. Potted palms greet me at the entrance and the doors slide back silently when I go up to them. In Reception there are enormous, leather covered sofas, and tables made from lush dark wood with glass tops, not a smear on them.

This is nothing like the places where I've worked before, with an office like a shed, some tacky furniture and a phone. This is a palace where everything is quality and so spotless there must be coachloads of cleaners going round all the time, wiping the floor after you've walked in and dusting the sofa after you've sat down. I half look round to see if I'm being tailed by one of these cleaners. I'm really glad I polished my shoes.

Two movie stars are sat behind a reception desk the size of a runway. Straightening my tie, I go up to the nearest one. 'Hi. I've… er… come for this job interview?' I show her the email from Madame de L'Étang.

She flashes me a smile that would shatter sunglasses. 'That's cool, Joe. Would you like a coffee while you wait?'

I really would like a coffee, as I didn't have any breakfast, and I'm about to say, 'That would be great.' But then I think, 'She's probably going to give me a kind of menu like you get in Starbucks, with latte, mocha, mocha with latte, mocha with choc shreds, and maybe mocha with spaghetti, and I don't want to look a complete pillock before I've even got into the interview.' So I say, 'I'm good, thanks,' and I wander over to one of these leather sofas, and sit down. And kind of slide backwards into it, it's so huge. I so hope that Dad's suit doesn't have Fats' cat hairs on it, otherwise there'll probably be ten cleaners on the case the moment I get up.

I try to imagine what Madame de L'Étang must look like. I guess that as she's a Madame she's married and probably has kids, and maybe they're grown up and live in France while she has a sophisticated lifestyle here in Bristol. Of course, she must have a lover, as French men and women do, and no one seems to mind, not even with politicians, Grandad says.

So I've got this image in my head of Helen Mirren with a French accent, when I see this tiny old lady with grey hair sort of swept up behind, a smart suit and high heels, click-clacking across from the lift. She looks quite severe, but as she comes up to me she puts on a smile. I struggle to get out of this slippery leather sofa, and now I'm two feet above her. I'd have to get down on my knees to shake hands with her. But she's clutching a clipboard, so I don't need to.

'It's Joe, isn't it?'

Well, I hope it is. She doesn't have any kind of a French accent; but then, neither does Mum, as she's lived in England for so long. 'Good to meet you, Madame.'

'Monsieur le Directeur is ready to see you now, Joe.'

We walk upstairs with carpets so soft you can't hear a thing, polished wood railings on either side. At the top, there's a door that's covered in more of this quality wood. Madame knocks, then opens it.

As we go in, I see another table like a runway and two sparkling glass chandeliers hanging from the ceiling. Must keep the cleaners busy changing the bulbs.

Then, I see Monsieur le Directeur. He's sitting at the end of the table but he gets up as I enter with Madame. His hair is so silver it seems to glitter in the light of the chandeliers, and it's cropped short, perfectly cut. He's slim but athletic-looking, like he works out regularly, and he's wearing a suit that I guess is Armani it looks so good. He has grey eyes, and his cheekbones are fine and chiselled. In fact, this guy really does look like I wouldn't mind looking, when I'm as old as he is.

Monsieur takes me in for maybe a second before he comes over with a slight smile, holding out his hand, and says in a quiet voice with a small trace of an accent, perhaps it's American, 'Joe, welcome. It's good to meet you. Have you been well looked after while you've been waiting?'

Hoping that the tiny pause didn't mean I have a snotty nose, I shake his hand, and feel a firm grip, with long fingers that wrap round mine. 'Yes, just fine thanks.' Then I think about how Mum says you talk to French people, and I say, 'Just fine, Monsieur le Directeur. Thank you.' I say the French words with an English accent. I don't want to look too clever because I know that doesn't work in job interviews.

He waves me over to the chair next to his and says to Madame, 'A light lunch as arranged, please Françoise, in twenty minutes.' She click-clacks off like a nervous little duck. Monsieur le Directeur sits down, so I do too. 'Tell me why you applied for this job, Joe.'

'It's the driving, Monsieur le Directeur.' Now I'm feeling really nervous. Will he suss my age?

He gives that half-smile again, 'Do I take it that driving is a pleasure for you?'

'When I saw that ad, it seemed like the job I've wanted all my life, Monsieur le Directeur.'

His grey eyes are looking straight at me now. 'I see that you have a French surname – St Aubin?'

'Er… yes. It's my mother's name – she's French.'

Monsieur's eyes are hawk-like. This is a man you do not want to lie to. Hoping that he doesn't ask why we don't use Dad's surname, I stare awkwardly at the table. But he just nods. 'And do you speak French, Joe?'

'A bit…' If I tell him that I'm not bad, he's going to start chatting in French and I won't be able to understand because French words just flow into each other.

'You have been to France?'

'Oh yes – Mum has friends in Aix-en-Provence…' I'm on safe ground now and as Monsieur knows Aix well, we have a really fun conversation until lunch arrives, carried in by two more starlets who are almost as stunning as the divas in Reception. It's Caesar salads, and fruit juice. I'm relieved because I was dreading it would be a four-course meal where I'd need sat nav to find the right knives and forks.

Monsieur le Directeur just picks at his Caesar while I try not to gulp mine down. Perhaps he's going for a fancy meal tonight with some real movie stars and wants to leave plenty of room for it.

When I've cleaned up my plateful he says thoughtfully, 'So, you like driving, Joe. Would you like to do some driving now, to show me what kind of chauffeur you would be for me?'

'Show me the car, and I'll show you my driving, Monsieur le Directeur.'

We leave this room and its glittering chandeliers, and we go into the lift outside in the corridor.

Monsieur touches a button labelled SS, and I remember that in French SS means sous-sol – below ground. The lift hisses down into the basement. As we walk out of it we seem to be in an underground carpark. It's lit partly by overhead lamps and partly by the daylight coming through two windows with bars that look out onto a street. I can just make out a silver Jag XKR and a yellow Lamborghini, Lenny's dream car. But I can't see anything else because it's so shadowy down here.

Then Monsieur says, in a casual kind of way, 'What would be your first thought if you had to get me away from a dangerous situation in this carpark, Joe? Assuming that there would be a car available?'

I'm not expecting this at all, but I remember that time in Bristol with Leah Wilks. 'The car would have to have a full tank.'

'And if the car had plenty of fuel and there was another car in here with people who are looking for us, what would you do?'

Now, my imagination's working overtime. 'I wouldn't use your car, not right away. We'd get right down underneath a different car, so their headlights wouldn't find us. They'd think we'd escaped, so they wouldn't waste any more time here. Then we get into your car, and go where you want to go.'

I hope I've passed my chauffeur's oral exam, although I don't think it was anything like the driving test is. I guess Monsieur must get chased around by the paparazzi all the time because he's so rich. He says, 'It's time for a little drive, Joe. In my favourite car.'

We leave the carpark and take the lift again, down to a floor below the basement. I always thought the sous-sol was the bottom floor. But not here at L'Étoile Fine Wines. We're in a cave. It's cold and damp. I can see rocky walls, and here in the darkness, lit only by a few lamps bolted onto the walls, there's rack on rack of bottles, and barrel on barrel of wines.

Monsieur le Directeur sees me looking at them. His quiet voice echoes slightly in the cave, as he says, 'My company imports quality wines by the barrel, Joe, which we bottle with the Étoile Fine Wines label. We also import really fine wines which my clients want to buy as investments because they'll be worth even more in a few years' time.'

Then Monsieur's voice becomes grave, and I can still remember every word he said. 'Of course, this cave hasn't always been used to store valuable wines, Joe, although it's so secure that it's ideal for it. Have you heard of the Bristol slave traders?'

I shake my head.

'They were rich merchants, who made their fortunes from importing and selling slaves. They continued to bring in thousands of slaves even after it became illegal. They used places like this underground cavern to keep them until they were taken secretly through tunnels up to Clifton to be sold.' He pauses, looking at me in the darkness, and I can't see his face. 'This place has a shameful past.'

It's not just the cold of the cave that's making me shiver as I look at the shadows that surround us. Monsieur goes on, in a more business-like tone, 'It's also where I keep my favourite car.'

I'm not cold anymore. It's a Bentley. A Continental. Just like the one in the ad. So some ads tell the truth, then. This huge, dramatic car with its big mesh grille is pale gold, and the sleek, aggressive lines just blow me away. It oozes power and speed and living on the edge of everything you could ever want. Monsieur le Directeur throws me the key. 'This is the driving part of the interview, Joe.'

I open the driver's door, and stare at the acres of wood and leather, not a crisp packet in sight. I slip into the driving seat, and touch the steering wheel with those flying wings in the centre. The smell of leather almost goes to my head. Nobody would dare eat a Pot Noodle in here, any more than they would in front of the Queen.

'Let me take you through the controls, Joe.' I wonder if he's going to give me a test on them. They're so complicated, they make my Peugeot look like something out of Toys R Us.

'Are you OK with all that, Joe?'

I swallow and nod. 'I think so, Monsieur.'

'Then, let's go.'

I press the starter button and there's the quiet rumble of a massive V12 engine. It sounds like a lion that would like to eat quite soon. But the lion's far away, just getting a sniff of its prey. I dab at the pedal like I'd play with a tiny kitten, and we're gliding forwards. This car is so big, it makes the cave seem like a cupboard; I'm terrified of scraping it along the stone walls. My hands are slippery on the leather steering wheel, and I ask myself why my first ever go in an automatic has to be in a machine that's got to be worth 250 times more than mine is.

Somehow, we make it to the exit. Two doors swish aside, leaving a space so narrow that I hold my breath. I inch the car along just waiting for the screech of metal. Then we're out near Bristol city centre, and I know where we are. Monsieur le Directeur says, 'Now, we head for Weston-super-Mare.'

It's amazing how the sight of a Bentley makes other drivers give way. I feel like a celebrity and wave my thanks as we slip through the traffic and onto the motorway. I'm in control of a Bentley Continental. Doing a regulation seventy mph in a car that can do an awful lot more. In a job interview that's more like being on Top Gear. And I haven't messed up yet.

'Do you feel comfortable with the car now, Joe?'

'It's a beast, Monsieur, but I think I'm getting to know it.'

'What do you see behind you?'

I've been watching it. 'There's a black Porsche Carrera, looking like it's going to overtake us.'

'Let's lose the Porsche, Joe.'

I give the accelerator a bit of a shove, and feel the kick in my back as we power away from the Porsche. It's suddenly very small in the rear view mirror, and we're doing a hundred and eighty. The car feels rock solid; it was born to do this speed. I feel like I was born to do it too.

Then Monsieur says, 'We have to leave at this junction.'

The exit is just a hundred yards away. With what Becks' brother Steve used to call, 'Enthusiastic braking, Joe', when he was teaching me, we come off the M5 in one piece. Five minutes later, I see a small sign on the right that says 'Private Road'.

'Take the right, Joe. We are almost there now.'

Private Road is incredibly narrow. A 30-tonne lorry with attitude coming the other way would not be good. We get to a barrier like the entrance to a carpark where there's a dude in this little office with a sliding window. The barrier lifts, and we drive on. There's just this road ahead with a parking area to one side. The road's really wide, like you could have six or seven cars driving along it side by side. And all around, it's completely flat.

Monsieur looks at me. 'There are no other vehicles here, Joe, and no police cameras. Now, I want you to show me how fast you can drive my favourite car.'

Hoping that my hearing isn't going and he hasn't said 'The last time you drive my favourite car', I floor the accelerator. I'm shunted back in the driving seat as the monster takes off, the scenery's flying past, and we're doing a hundred and eighty again. The engine sounds like it's spotted its prey, the lion's purring happily.

Then I hear warning bells in my head, as I see the start of a bend. I'm easing off a bit, when Monsieur says, 'You don't have to slow down, Joe. Trust the car.'

So I trust Monsieur and I trust the car. I keep on the power and we're going into the bend. It's one long arc, and there's not a sound from those fat tyres. We get through the bend without coming unstuck, and I know exactly what I can see ahead of me now and I know what kind of road we're on. It's a chicane ahead and we're on a test track. I've seen them when I was watching Top Gear with Steve, and I remember how he said you have to take a chicane.

I hold my breath and power in, brakes hard on, let the tail slide, swing the wheel the opposite way you normally would, and power out. Again, and again. The tyres are chatting away but they sound happy. And this huge car is behaving just as I'm praying it will. Monsieur is quiet beside me, and I can't see what colour his knuckles are. We're through the chicane, and we're heading into another straight, doing nearly two hundred mph. I've never driven at half this speed before; I can hear the grey cells babbling in my brain. Then we're hurtling towards what looks like a load of gravel on the road; it seems to go on and on, and I think, 'Don't, whatever you do, touch the brakes!'

That's when Monsieur says, 'Stop now, Joe.'

So I do what every instinct is screaming at me not to. I stamp on the brake pedal, and keep my foot there. The tyres are really shouting now. They're yelling as loud as my instincts and I can feel the ABS pumping through the brake pedal. The seatbelt's biting into my ribs and my stomach's trying for a quick exit through my throat. I can see smoke in the rear view mirror – must be coming from the tyres – but the Bentley's going in a dead straight line. Gravel is flying around and I cringe in case some of it hits us.

We've stopped. The engine's still growling quietly, like it's just had a stroll through the jungle but didn't find lunch after all. My heart's making far more noise than the engine. But it's not like I feel scared.

I look at Monsieur. He's sitting there with not a sleek silver hair out of place. That half-smile is there again. 'What do you think of my favourite car, Joe?'

I try to sound as cool as he is. 'I think I could handle that chicane a bit better next time. Can I take your favourite car round again, Monsieur le Directeur?'

'That will not be necessary, Joe. You have shown me all I need to see.'

Half an hour later, we turn into the cave.

'We will go back up to my office for the final part of the interview, Joe.'

I park, and this time it's so easy, but I think, 'How do I turn the engine off?' Then, I remember that I need to push a button on the dashboard, and while I'm fumbling around for it, I must have hit the driver's window switch, because the window glides down.

I stare at it. It's not like the kind of glass that's in my Peugeot. The window glass in Monsieur le Directeur's Precious is an inch thick. My brain does a quick Control S, as I hit the switch to get the window back up.

I don't know if Monsieur notices or not. He slips out of the passenger seat, and heads for the lift. I go back up by the stairs, thinking, 'This is what chauffeurs do, we take the stairs while the boss takes the lift.'

We meet outside those doors, and go back into the room with the chandeliers. As I hand him back the key I wonder if I've done anything like as well as all the other interviewees who've driven round that test track.

Monsieur's on the phone to Madame de L'Étang. 'Be so good as to send Patrice up to us please, Françoise.' She comes in, followed by a dude carrying measuring tape and a notebook, and he tells me to stand still and raise my arms, while he runs the tape over practically every part of my body.

Monsieur says, 'And now we get to the part of the interview where you can ask the questions, Joe. So, what would you like to know about the job?'

As Patrice measures my neck with cold hands I ask about the pay. Monsieur nods, as though I should have asked much earlier. He names a monthly amount that's four times what I'm on now. 'Do you have any more questions, Joe? Feel free to ask.'

I take a deep breath. 'When will I know if you're going to offer me the job, Monsieur le Directeur?'

He shrugs – it's the first thing he's done that looks really French. 'Patrice would not be measuring you up for your chauffeur's uniform if we had no intention of offering you the job, Joe.'

Monsieur le Directeur has gone to make some phone calls. My head's spinning with a weird feeling. This must be Happiness; not Hope, but the Real Deal. I have to swallow hard to get the words out. 'When does Monsieur want me to start, Madame?'

'Tomorrow, Joe. We will find you an acceptable chauffeur's uniform, until your own is ready.'

'That's fantastic, Madame. What time does Monsieur want me to be here?' I'm thinking about what bus I'll need to get to Bristol. She calls him, and after a few minutes, he comes in.

'Do you have your own transport, Joe?'

'Well, I do, but it's not driveable right now. But it's cool, I can take the bus, Monsieur.'

Monsieur is quiet for a moment, looking at me, and I can't guess what he's thinking. Then he puts his hand in his pocket and throws me a key. I just about catch it, and stare. It's the key to the Bentley.

My brain's sending me all kinds of messages, like 'This program has performed an illegal act and will be shut down.' I hear myself say, 'Monsieur le Directeur, I love this car, it's amazing, but it could get trashed outside my house. We'd never get it into the garage.'

He's still looking at me in a way that I can't work out. 'See it as one of the perks of the job, Joe. As for the possible risks – that's why we have insurance. Take the car. And be here at seven tomorrow morning.'

He shakes my hand again with those long fingers. 'Welcome to L'Étoile Fine Wines, Joe.' Then, almost like a throwaway, with that half-smile, 'I very much enjoyed our drive.'

CHAPTER 6

Heaven

'Oh-my-God, Joe – what have you done now?' Becks stares at Monsieur's favourite car. 'I don't believe this!'

Steve comes out of the house, and gives a low whistle as he takes in The Beast.

I've rehearsed this, all the way from Bristol to Becks' place, and it still feels like I've got the wrong script. 'It's only a matter of months before I'll be legal, Becks. I couldn't pass it up – a chance like this could never come my way again.'

'You must be out of your head! What if you get caught again? Don't you think of your mum at all?'

My face goes hot and I don't know what to say.

Steve walks around Monsieur's Precious, runs a hand across the gleaming gold paintwork, sits at the wheel and inhales the leather. Nods. 'Quite an animal, eh, Joe?'

Becks shakes her head, green eyes blazing. 'What IS it with dudes and cars? Tell him he's an idiot, Steve!'

'You're an idiot, Joe. An' I want your job.'

'You're a pair of STUPID GREAT KIDS!' Becks storms back into the house, banging the door behind her, as net curtains right and left start to flutter. Like stupid great kids do, Steve and I carry on as though nothing's happened.

'Thanks for letting me doss with you tonight, Steve. I've told Mum I'm here, and that I got the job. I just couldn't say…'

He grins. '…what the job is. You're a quality driver, Joe. Not your fault if the rules don't allow for early developers. Just be careful, that's all.'

There's no sign of Becks when we go in.

'Better let her cool off. She'll come round.'

I'm not so sure about that. Especially when the front door opens then bangs shut again a few minutes later. She still hasn't come back when I crash out on their sofa at half ten.

When I wake up at five the next morning, I'm soaked with sweat. I'm convinced that either I've imagined the whole thing, or the Bentley's real but someone's poured acid over it and kicked the panels in. And the whole night, I've been dreaming about Becks chucking bucket loads of brown paint over me. At least, I think it was paint.

Lenny's left a message on my voicemail: 'Hi Joe. How's your Grandad? Go see a film tonight?'

I drive sedately back to Bristol wearing Dad's Balmain, trying to look really old, at least thirty, like a re-habbed rock star with his new toy. It's a relief as Precious glides quietly into the cave. I haven't phoned Lenny. I don't know how to tell him I've got the job that he warned me off so urgently.

In a room next to Madame's office Patrice has a rail full of uniforms for me to try on. He holds a jacket up against my chest, and tuts. 'You 'ave very broad shoulders, Monsieur Joe. Do you work out?'

'Only with Big Macs.'

He takes another jacket off the rail. 'I am not sure thees will be long enough, you are so tall.'

Patrice is the first person I've met in this place who has a French name and a French accent to go with it. I'm trying on the fourth uniform when Madame knocks. 'Monsieur le Directeur would like to see you in his office, Joe, when convenient.' I know that 'when convenient' actually means 'like, now', because you don't keep your boss waiting. Patrice is fussing around, and this uniform's about OK, just a bit tight under the armpits.

'Look, I really have to go.' I'm trying to button up the jacket, when Patrice takes this chauffeur's cap and jams it on my head. It bounces off my thick crew cut, I grab it, 'Thanks, Patrice,' and leg it for the stairs.

As I get to the top of the stairs I see a big dude in another Armani suit heading out of Monsieur's office and into the lift. All I glimpse is his bulky shape, big head and sticking out ears, before he's gone.

Monsieur is there, behind the runway. 'Sit down, Joe. There's something I need to discuss with you.'

I hope that I've not made some stupid mistake, like wearing a uniform that's too tight, or using the wrong deodorant, or having bad breath.

Personal hygiene isn't what he wants to talk about. 'I've been considering your situation living at home, Joe. Many of our journeys will be at anti-social hours. And there will be times when I will need you to be instantly available, not a half-hour drive away. So, I think it would be better if you live here, in our offices. You would have your own apartment, there are several within this building. Naturally, the company would pay all the costs. How do you feel about my proposition?'

Of course I say, 'That would be great, Monsieur le Directeur.' Even if I didn't fancy living in a free apartment in the centre of Bristol, with all the night-life around me, and shops and restaurants and cinemas, I'd still have said Yes. Because I've learned one big thing in a short time: you don't say No to Monsieur le Directeur. If I reply, 'Actually I'd rather live at home, thanks', this heaven that I've found will implode and I'll be back with Lenny in that no-hope job with my family telling me how to live my life. I'll be a loser again.

So I smile my biggest smile. 'It'll be amazing to live here in my own apartment, Monsieur. But can I have some choice as to the drapes?'

He smiles too, that half-smile again. 'I think you mean the curtains, Joe.' He shakes his head in mock disapproval. 'You have been watching too much American TV.'

I don't think you can watch too much American TV, but I don't say so. 'And will there be broadband, and Sky, Monsieur?'

He replies, in mock resignation this time, 'Yes, Joe, there will be broadband and Sky in your apartment. Madame will show you round.'

This job is getting more like heaven with every minute. And I think, 'There's a logical explanation for that thick window glass. Every important person needs it, don't they? They have to protect themselves. Perhaps that dude with the big head I saw leaving the office just now is Monsieur's minder.'

—m—

The apartment's on the second floor and it's probably bigger than my house. There are vertical blinds at the windows, so no worries about posh flowery drapes. The vast lounge is like the backdrop to the photos they take of celebrities in their homes when they've just had a baby or got divorced. There's acres of thick grey carpet, small runways for tables, and sofas that aren't leather – thank you, Monsieur – just soft cushions that you can collapse into with a can of Coke, very carefully. The massive widescreen TV with DVD player has got Sky, like Monsieur said it would. And there's a PC with broadband, right next to the TV.

The kitchen is like a Jamie Oliver film set, all pale creamy wood, with a microwave to heat up my lasagne ready meal, and a cooker that looks like a space ship with its gleaming metal and hood. In the bathroom, there's a shower that sprays water over you from just about all directions, and loads of soft, white towels.

'Is there a washing machine, Madame?'

'You will not need one, Joe. There is a laundry service to take care of everything.' Mum says that too, but with a different tone of voice.

In the bedroom, there's a king-sized double bed, and lights over the bedside tables, so I can read up on maps to work out where I'm going next. 'This is amazing, Madame, I'm going to love it here.'

I take in the view of the docks through the blue-tinted windows. 'How do I get back in here, Madame, like when I go out during my time off?'

'I will get you a key, Joe, that will let you in at the back and up the stairs so that you won't set off the burglar alarm. But you must lock and bolt the door behind you, every time.' She closes the apartment door quietly behind her.

As I'm trying out all the channels on Sky and looking for Top Gear, an error message pops up in my mind. If Monsieur wants me to live in this apartment, so I'm available 24/7, does that mean he lives here too? Somewhere in this office block, in one of the other apartments?

I don't think so. Doesn't fit with that sleek, silver hair, chiselled face and Armani suit. He must live in a billionaire's mansion up in Clifton. So, why does he want me to live here, and not in his mansion? Then I think, well, he keeps Precious here, so it makes sense for me to be here too. When he calls me up in the middle of the night, I'll drive up to his place to collect him. Wonder what it's like, Monsieur's place.

My mobile goes, and the voice brings me down to earth with a bump. 'The date for the trial is set for December 2nd, Joe. I've informed your mother. I'd like to meet up with you before then to talk over a few things.'

'I've got a job, Inspector, and I'm like on call all hours, so a meeting's a bit tricky at the moment… but it's probably very temporary. Maybe only a week or so.'

'The meeting needs to be within the next few weeks, Joe. We have to be one hundred percent clear on the facts, and so do you'.

'I'll call you in a couple of days, when I know how long they want me for – that OK, Inspector?' I'm so relieved DIW doesn't ask about the job.

I call Becks. 'Sorry, can't talk to you right now. The funnier your message, the sooner I'll get back to you.'

I can't think of anything funny. 'Becks, I'm really sorry. Please, let's talk?'

Then, I brace myself for the phone call home. I daren't tell Mum and Grandad about this apartment; they're bound to think there's a catch, because it's so just too good to be true. I'll make up for all these lies one day, when I'm really successful in my new job, and they can be proud of me.

'How was your first day, love? Did it go well?'

'Really well, Mum. But the commute's going to cost a bomb. So, one of the guys I'm working with says his parents can let me doss in their spare room?'

'Oh.' The excitement in her voice gives way to the worried note. 'Can you come home at weekends?'

'Probably not, as I'm working shifts. But the job's not for long.'

'How long is 'not for long'?'

'Maybe just a couple of weeks. And it's really brilliant. My boss is so cool. That OK, Mum?'

Mum sighs. I know she wants to say 'No way'. But she hates party-pooping with me and Jack. 'Well... all right... but you will keep in touch, won't you, love? Text me with the address of where you're working. And where you're staying. And take care, promise?'

'Promise. Love you Mum.'

—m—

Steve collects my stuff from home and brings it down in the afternoon, in return for a French lesson. He taught me to drive in return for me teaching him some French as he has a French girlfriend. I open the door and he takes a step back, almost dropping the suitcases. 'Blimey, you look like the Gestapo. Sieg Heil, mein Fuhrer!' He snaps his heels together.

I'm annoyed to feel my face going red. 'It's only what every chauffeur wears. If they drive a Bentley, anyway.' I take one of the suitcases as we go inside.

'You just need the black leather boots.' He looks round, picks up the TV remote, presses a button and inspects the HD screen, as Rooney slams the ball home. 'Now that telly is quality. Cool flat, Joe.' I take him on a guided tour.

'How on earth d'you work the shower? Looks like a secret weapon.'

'How's Becks? She's not answering.'

'If I was you, I'd try radio silence for a few days, mate. Now, what's the French for 'You look really great in that dress, Annette'?'

CHAPTER 7

Servant and Master

After Steve's gone, I change into jeans and nip out for a Chinese. A forkload of sweet and sour is on its way into my mouth when Madame calls. 'There is a consignment of wine for delivery this evening, Joe. Can you please be in my office in five minutes.'

I put the fork down, puzzled. I thought it was Monsieur I would be driving. They've got delivery vans for the wine, haven't they? Then I think, well, it is fine wines. Monsieur's customers must expect a really five star service. They'll get that alright, with the most expensive delivery van on the planet.

Battling with the stiff buttons, I scramble back into my uniform, and check in the mirror for any food that could have sneakily plopped onto my chin. I just make it to Madame's office in time. It's half eight at night; Madame must work flexible hours, like me. She's sat at her desk, tearing a sheet of paper from a notepad. 'The consignment is in the boot of the Bentley, Joe. It is to go to this Kensington address, for ten o'clock.' She hands over the piece of paper.

'Do I ask them to pay, or sign for it, or anything?'

She shakes her head. 'There is no need. Come straight back; there may be another delivery when you return.'

As I leave her office, I'm even more baffled. Another delivery after this one? It'll be well gone midnight by then. These customers can't be in nine to five jobs. Will a dude meet me at the door in his pyjamas, or what?

Butterflies are bobbing in my stomach as I take the lift two floors down to where Precious is waiting, gold coachwork glowing in the dimly lit cave. By the time I slip into the leather-scented cabin, I'm tingling all over. Should I take a look in the boot, just to check that the wine's there? Better not. Don't want to be late on my first run.

The lion wakes, and gurgles quietly. We glide forwards, the headlights blazing into the cave, I hit the remote and the doors swish open. With quite a bit more confidence than I had on that first drive with Monsieur, I ease the Bentley out into the street, look right – and jam on the brakes as my heart leaps into my throat. There's a police car coming towards me. My chauffeur's career could be so short, it'll make the Guinness Book of Records. The driver flashes me to go ahead. But my heart's thumping all the way onto the M4, and at every junction, my head whizzes round like an owl.

Damn, I've forgotten to put the address into the sat nav. At the services I pull over, and look at the crumpled piece of paper, trying to get my head back together. It's difficult to read Madame's spidery writing. Number 26… what's the name of the street? Burlington or Darlington? I'll go for Burlington. My stomach knots up, as I remember the last time I had a problem with street names. I tell myself, 'Get a grip, that was then.'

The sat nav likes Burlington; it fits with the postcode I've keyed in. 'Please press OK to confirm address.' Those sugary female tones with their Texas twang are going to get changed when I get back. I wonder if the voice menu has a Top Gear option…'At the next left, make a handbrake turn.'

'Yeah, Jeremy.'

The rest of the trip to Kensington goes without any more heart-stoppers. My American girlfriend talks me patronizingly to number 26, Burlington Drive; there's even a parking space just outside the tall, elegant house, with its black railings, white-painted door, and polished brass knocker. The Bentley's in quite good company with a dark blue Ferrari in front of us and a silver Mercedes SL Coupe behind, gleaming in the street lights.

Jamming on my cap I open the boot. There are two wooden cases with labels bearing the L'Étoile Fine Wines logo; the intricate, sixteen-point star that I first saw on that ad. A larger wooden box is behind them. This one has no label: is it more wine, or something else? I tuck the labelled cases under each arm – they feel heavy enough to contain wine bottles – as I take the steps three at a time up to that brass knocker. There's a doorbell on the right so I press it; I guess the knocker's just there for show. I can't hear the bell ring inside the house. What do I do now? Press it again, or try knocking?

Maybe a minute ticks past, and I'm just about to try the bell again, when the door opens. I can hear a buzz of voices somewhere beyond, as a young dude appears in the doorway. He must be around twenty. He's got blond hair that flops over his eyes and he's wearing a black evening suit, kind of casually, like Bond. The white shirt is open at the collar, the bow tie dangling either side.

'I'll take those. Get the rest.' His crisp, cold voice sounds like he went to an expensive school, where they learn to give orders but not to say Thanks.

I hand over the wine cases, and go back down the steps for the third box. It's lighter than the others. Perhaps it's wine glasses. As I approach the door again, he's waiting outside this time. In the street lights his face is easier to see now. The skin is taut over his cheekbones and jaw, and there are frown lines between his eyebrows that make him look older than he is. He almost snatches the box. They must all be gagging for a glass of expensive wine in there.

He stares at me. 'Well, what are you waiting for?'

'Is… is that OK, then?'

'Just get lost, idiot.' The door swings shut behind him.

My feet are wooden, almost tripping me over as I make my way slowly down the steps and back into Precious's leather seat. I start up the engine, and glance in my mirror to check behind me. A middle-aged couple in evening wear are going up the steps to number 26. Even at night, I can see they have a Bermuda tan. Jewels around the woman's neck flash as she picks her way upwards, holding her long dress.

A horn blasts impatiently behind me. A crimson Daimler is indicating left to pull into my parking space. Precious glides out of it, and I can see the peaked cap of their chauffeur pointing backwards and forwards, as he manoeuvres the limo into the slot. He's going to have to sit there, waiting like a dog tied up outside a supermarket for hours, maybe all night, till his owners are ready to go home. If I was him, I'd have brought my iPod with me. But I saw white hair under that black cap; he's more likely going to have a quiet snooze.

I pull into a bus stop, and switch on the sat nav. The main menu comes up as Barbie Doll trills, 'Welcome to the world of GoPlaces. You don't know the place, so we go there together.'

I growl back at her, 'You don't know it yet, but you've been sacked.'

The lights are out in Madame's office when I tap on the door. No more deliveries tonight, then. She's left a note for me on her desk. 'Please tell the security guard that he can lock up, Joe. Do not go out again tonight. The alarms will be on.'

What security guard? I jump, as a shadow falls over the piece of paper.

'You finished for the night, then?'

The voice is gruff, but not unfriendly. I look beyond the uniform, at bright blue eyes in a lined face, and see a wiry figure that looks fit enough to chase off any unwanted company. He's carrying a torch and a two-way radio.

'Yeah, I'm done, thanks. Just going up to my flat.'

He's locking Madame's office, and I'm about to go up the stairs, when I think, I'm probably going to meet up with this guy again, as they seem to go in for night deliveries in my new job. Hesitantly, I hold out my hand. 'My name's Joe.'

He could just tell me to Get Lost, Idiot. But a strong, bony hand clasps mine in return, although the voice is as rough-edged as before. 'They told me you'd be late in. Get up to your flat now, son. And don't leave before six, or there'll be all hell with the alarms.'

I plod back up to my posh apartment, peel off the black jacket and chuck my hat on the sofa. I can't work out whether I'm more hungry than tired, or the other way. I give my Chinese a blast in the microwave, and sit down with it on my lap to stare at footie. When I wake up at four in the morning Home Alone is playing on Sky, and my hand that was holding the fork has flopped into my cold plate of sweet and sour.

—〰—

Over the next few days, I leave more messages for Becks. Still can't make them funny. Still no call back. Is she OK? Perhaps she's ill, maybe even in hospital. Should I call Steve? But he would have contacted me, wouldn't he? It's so not like Becks to stay this angry with me. Even when I fell off the roof of that bus shelter in Stroud after Jack dared me to climb it, she was only cross for a day. We've never been out of touch for this long.

Checking for a message from Becks every time I stop, I do drops to Leeds, Manchester and Newcastle. All the deliveries are at night. All the faces look at me like I have some kind of infectious disease and they can't wait to close the door. I do Kensington again. At number 26, Burlington Drive, it's a different guy who takes the boxes this time. He looks at me like I'm a Tesco You Shop, We Drop driver, and he's not interested in what I hand over to him.

At nine thirty, the morning after that drop, I don't throw the alarm clock at the wall. I'm fed up with being out all night and then sleeping all day, like Fats does. I crawl out of bed, and blast open my glued-shut eyes with the power shower on nuke setting. Then I make myself a Mum-style fry-up, and burn the bacon while I watch Clarkson blowing up some car he loves to hate. I'm trying to scrub off baked beans that have splatted onto the roof of the microwave, when the phone rings. 'Are you available to drive me to Plymouth, Joe?'

Like, of course I'm available. Monsieur's my boss, isn't he? I dive into my uniform like I'm jet-propelled. He sits in the front seat, cool as ever in the black Armani. As I key in the address, and the English voice announces solemnly, 'Destination confirmed', he looks at me with that half-smile. 'It is preferable to the American, Joe. So, no more drapes, then?'

'There was a French option, Monsieur. But my French isn't that good.'

We fly down the motorway in the purring Precious, and I bombard Monsieur with questions about the TV screens in the head rests, the mood lighting, the automatic headlights and the rain sensing wipers, like this is a Bentley edition of Top Gear. He smiles as he tells me about his favourite car.

He doesn't ask how the deliveries are going, and now I don't care. Every job has its downside, doesn't it? I can live with dropping off cases of fine wines to people who've never learned how to say Thanks.

After a short wait for Monsieur outside a bank in a Plymouth high street, he tells me to follow signs to the marina. We park up and I follow him past the rows of moored yachts with their tinkling rigging. He stops when we get to a graceful white yacht, maybe sixty feet long, with a single, tall mast. Her name is painted in gold and black on the hull, in a flowing script. 'Lisette.' At the sight of her I start to tingle all over.

Monsieur adjusts the mooring so that it's ready to cast off, then swings himself onto the deck. I follow, my heart thumping with excitement. This could be as amazing as my first drive in the Bentley.

He checks the rigging before going into the cabin, returning with lifejackets and harnesses. 'Have you sailed before, Joe?'

'Only in our dinghy, with Grandad.'

'Dinghies are harder work. Now, you need to clip yourself onto the rail. '

I notice he's done the same. 'Is it going to get rough?'

'The forecast is for light winds, force two to three. But you should always be tethered. Sailing is an unpredictable business.' He starts the engine while I cast off and tidy the rope away. Slowly, the Lisette moves backwards off her mooring, and Monsieur steers her expertly through all the hundreds of yachts, catamarans and trimarans thronging the busy harbour. Suddenly, he swings the wheel hard left. A dark blue launch shoots across our bow to join another one at the harbour side. Uniformed officers swarm onto a gleaming Sunseeker cruiser. Monsieur sees me staring. 'The harbour police. Very likely they are searching for drugs.'

I swallow. 'What sort of drugs?'

His voice is severe. 'Cocaine, mostly.'

Soon we're clear of all the shipping and out in the open sea, with gulls crying piercingly over the top of that tall mast. 'Take the helm, Joe. I'm going to hoist the jib.'

Apprehensively, I take over the wheel. 'Is it like using a tiller?'

'It is easier. Just look ahead, not at the wheel.'

The jib unfurls and snaps as it catches the breeze. Then the mighty main is inched up the mast, and Monsieur turns off the engine as the Lisette moves smoothly through the small waves.

'Do you get to sail very often, Monsieur?'

He's gazing across the sea, in the direction of France. 'Very seldom, Joe. But as my business with the bank was quickly concluded, I felt that you and I deserved this little treat. Watch the main – the wind is changing direction.'

I look upwards at the soaring mast and see the main starting to flap. 'Which way should I turn her?'

'The same as in your dinghy – closer into the wind.'

I twitch the wheel and instantly the main is fat with air again. The Lisette puts on a spurt like the Bentley on a run.

'You learn quickly, Joe.'

'I wish they thought that at school, Monsieur.'

'School can teach you very little about life, Joe.'

For all the rest of that wonderful sail, staring at the horizon with my hands on the wheel, I'm in a kind of dream. Because in my mind's eye I'm seeing that white yacht that Dad was waving to from the suspension bridge when I had that strange wardrobe moment. Is this the same yacht? Am I sailing with the man who waved back to Dad? The colleague that Mum said had sailed over from Marseille? But even if I dared to ask, I'm not sure where I'd begin.

Later that day, after we've had a fantastic meal in a posh restaurant, and we're cruising at a careful 70 on the M5, I try to come at the questions I really want to ask, in a kind of roundabout way. 'The place where I park the Bentley, Monsieur. Is it a real cave? Like, it's so far underground?'

He replies like he was expecting me to ask, sometime. 'It was a real cave, once, Joe. There are many on the way to Blackboy Hill, where the slaves were sold. They are all connected by an underground trail, much of it made by human hands.'

'Did the slave traders make the trail?'

His voice is cold now. 'They would not have dirtied their pampered skin to do such work. Or face such danger. Many slaves died, carrying out that dreadful task.'

I feel bad, like I should have known. 'They've never mentioned any of that in my History GCSE.'

His face lit by the stream of oncoming headlights, he looks at the road, without really seeing it. 'It is not something to be proud of, Joe. The slaves would arrive on stinking ships, after terrible journeys, where thousands of them died of hunger or disease, or were thrown overboard, because they had become ill.'

'Didn't the police know about the slave traders, Monsieur? If it was illegal by then, couldn't they have arrested them, and set the slaves free?'

He shakes his head slowly. 'The merchants were rich

and powerful, beyond the reach of the forces of law and order. The abomination went on for years after the law was passed. Men, women and tiny children, snatched from their homeland, and marched up through those caverns. With no future ahead of them, except either dying on the way, or spending the rest of their lives belonging to someone else.'

The conversation has taken such a different tack that now I have no way of getting it round to Dad and the yacht.

—⚹—

When I'm back in my flash apartment, slumped in front of the TV and clutching a Coke, I can't help thinking about what Monsieur has said. Underneath the foundations of this glamorous, blue-glass office block is a hell-hole where people struggled, starved and died long ago, with no hope. Powerful and merciless criminals caused that misery. Maybe they weren't that different from the kind of criminals who Dad is fighting now, somewhere far away. And he is, because I refuse to believe that he's dead.

I wonder what Monsieur really feels about this ancient darkness beneath us. Perhaps, in some strange way that he tells no one about, he's fighting this kind of evil too. Suddenly, I almost drop the Coke can. I fish Dad's photo out of a drawer and stare at it; but it's not his dancing blue eyes that take centre stage now. Monsieur's hair is dark in the photo, but there's no mistaking those grey eyes and that half-smile. Now I'm sure that I'm working for the man who was a friend of my dad.

CHAPTER 8

Big Head

The next afternoon I drive a passenger to Birmingham. It's the dude with the big head, who I saw leaving the room with the chandeliers on my first day in my new job. Unlike Monsieur, he takes the back seat, and he never says a word to me all the way. He doesn't care about being overheard on his mobile, although I can't make much sense of it. He keeps on about 'That woman' and how 'time is running out'. The worst bit is when he lights up a cigar and stinks out the whole car; I resolve to give the Bentley a huge spring clean when we get back.

The house he's visiting is in a really run down part of the city. The streets are littered with old newspaper, and kids who look eleven years old are sat smoking on the pavement with their feet in the gutter. The building itself has a broken window upstairs, and the garden is full of dog poo. From somewhere inside, there's a persistent barking. Big Head opens the front door with his key and goes in. Keeping a close eye on those kids in case one of them decides that it would be a laugh to key the Bentley, I wait for a good twenty minutes.

As Big Head comes out, I get the shock of my life when I see the face looking out of a ground floor window.

It's half hidden behind the ragged curtain, but it makes me go cold, it looks so like Leah Wilks. In a flash, it's gone, and I tell myself, 'Get a grip, it can't be her.' All the same, it gives me some bad dreams that night.

The next day, I drive Big Head to the Kensington address. He's just as silent, and he must have got through ten cigars by the time we get to that posh house with the brass knocker. I watch him disappear through the front door. After he's gone, I open all the windows and sit there in a haze of smoke. Now, I'm not quite sure whether Big Head is Monsieur's minder or not. Unless he's checking out the security, in case Monsieur visits his clients here? I run my finger along the inch thick surface of the window glass, wondering if anyone's ever fired at the Bentley. Suddenly, someone's face appears right in front of mine and I recoil; it's the dude who took the last delivery at this place. 'You're not needed. Just get back.'

All the way back to the blue-glass office, the question of Big Head nags at me. The kind of swaggering way he acts, it's as if he's not an employee at all. And there's something creepy about him; I don't like being on my own with him in the Bentley. In the underground car park, I open all the doors and wipe the leather upholstery to try and get rid of the smell of cigar smoke. I'll have to put my uniform in the wash, as that stinks as well.

As I climb the stairs from the cave, my curiosity about Big Head gets too much, and instead of going up to my flat, I stop outside that room with the chandeliers. The door is ajar. I listen, and there's no sound. Pushing the door gently open, I tiptoe in and look around. A few papers lie on the huge expanse of the gleaming mahogany table, but they just look like invoices, with the 16-point star logo of L'Etoile Fine Wines. They're held down by a crystal paperweight that's the same star design. It's such a beautiful thing that I can't help picking it up and taking it to the window to gaze at its flashing rainbow lights. Cool and weighty in my hand, it glows with an inner fire.

Putting it carefully back, I look around the room once more. Apart from those invoices, there's no sign that Monsieur runs his business from here – not even a computer or a phone. And you'd expect maybe a personal photo, although he's never mentioned that he has family. In fact, Monsieur never talks about himself at all. So just where is his office if it's not here? Madame has her office, and you'd think it would be next door to his. And what about Big Head? He behaves like he's important enough to have an office of his own. Wondering if I might dare to ask Claire or Justine in Reception about all this, I slip quietly back up to my flat.

―⁂―

At eleven that night, I'm sat in my kitchen, eating a bacon buttie, too tired to take off my smelly uniform. I call Becks again. At last, she answers, her voice full of sleep. 'Joe, sorry… I got your messages, but I've been up to my eyes in coursework.'

I cling onto her words like a lifeline. She's not talking Stupid Great Kid. 'How's it going? Your art project was looking so brilliant.'

'Tracy Emin, look out!'

'And the Eng Lit? Wordsworth, wasn't it?'

'Byron. I'm getting a bit fed up with him. Too attention-seeking. And his poetry wasn't that much.'

Her bright voice in my head, I look around my flash, empty apartment. I can see her impatiently brushing strands of red hair away from her ears. 'Don't work too hard.'

She starts to sound a bit like my mum. 'What about your English coursework, Joe? You've got an awful lot of catch-up to do.'

'I'm putting some deep thought into Raymond Chandler... when there's time.'

I try to sound casual, but Becks has picked up like she has radar. 'How's the job? Boss OK?'

'He's well OK. There's just...'

'What?'

'Something... I can't put my finger on...'

'Have you seen any more of that dude who gatecrashed you in the hospital, Joe? Is that it?'

'No, nothing like that. It's cool, Becks, really.' I haven't told her about the cinema ambush because I don't want to worry her. I haven't reported it to DIW either, in spite of what he told me to do, because he might ask some uncomfortable questions about this job.

'Steve says your flat's awesome. Can I come visit?'

'Tomorrow?'

'Can't tomorrow. Deadline for History coursework. Thursday?'

'Thursday. Take care.'

'You take care, Joe. Big Sister is watching you, OK?'

In the background, I can hear Steve shouting, 'Becks! Put the phone down, I've got this internet game all lined up for eleven thirty!'

As I switch off my mobile, the phone in my flat rings. Five minutes later, I'm in Reception, and one of the movie stars is there too. Madame says briskly, 'Joe, we have orders that there is an urgent delivery for you to make with Justine. The Kensington address. You need to be there in ninety minutes.'

I'll never know how women in such high heels can move so fast without breaking their ankles. The Bentley's sliding out of the cave, Justine's sat herself in the front seat with one endless leg folded over the other, and I'm almost gasping in this fog of Chanel Number 25, or whatever it is. Bet Becks would know. Or maybe not, as this perfume smells just so expensive. But I'm used to it now. I've been in and out of Reception so many times, and the movie stars seem to like chatting with me. Must be the uniform. Becks says, 'A uniform always makes dudes look good as they have no idea how to dress otherwise.' Steve didn't think so. But he doesn't know everything.

We cruise along the M4 at a speed that's totally boring for Monsieur's Precious but fast enough to get us there on time, unless there's a really big problem when we hit London. I tune in to the Traffic Alert system which has these cameras on the motorway, sending signals to a control centre that tells you where the jams are.

Then Justine says, and she's never had any kind of a French accent either, 'Are you liking your new job then, Joe?'

'I love it, and the car is so cool.'

'You don't mind working all hours?'

'I like driving at night. People aren't quite so stupid when it's dark. What are we delivering, then?'

'Oh, just a couple of cases of Pomerol, Chateau Petrus 1995. Worth around thirteen thousand. Our client had to have that year, and we just happened to have it in stock. He wants it tonight. So, here we are.'

On all the runs I've done, no one ever talked money. 'That's an awful lot of dosh for twelve bottles of wine, isn't it?'

Justine shrugs, and she does look a bit French now. 'Of course, it's not just the wine he's ordered. We're bringing the accessories as well.'

'What are the accessories?'

She looks at me like I'm an eleven year-old kid, and not driving her at eighty mph in this Bentley that's worth a quarter of a million pounds. 'Well, you know, the cigars.' Then she says the next words like she just can't resist, 'And the rest.' And she laughs and laughs, like she's made a really brilliant joke.

I can hear the young dude's cold voice saying, 'Get the rest.' And Justine's eyes, when I glance at her, look so bright and shining in the light from passing headlights. But her face is pale, in spite of all that movie star make-up. I can see a trickle of sweat on her forehead, beneath that blonde, tightly combed-back hair. Justine's not a movie star anymore; she's someone I don't know at all.

Maybe she thinks I know what she means with The Accessories. Monsieur has never mentioned cigars. Although I guess it makes sense. Fine cigars and fine wines, they go together, don't they? But what is The Rest?

My voice is croaky, deeply uncool. 'The traffic information system's telling me there's a jam near

Kensington. We'll have to take a detour round the back streets. We should still get there on time, no worries.' But I am worrying.

Justine has gone quiet. No more laughter. She just dabs at her face with a tissue, still looking pale. It's like, the movie script has been changed, but no one's told me. I'm paralysed with the script changing like this, because my part could have changed too. But I have no idea how.

We get to the house, and I open the boot of the Bentley. There's the wine case with the Pomerol. And, as usual, there's the bigger wooden boxes, two of them this time, like the ones I've delivered before. Justine grabs one of them. I see how easily she picks it up. I take the case of Pomerol up the steps towards the white-painted door with its shiny brass knocker, and we stand there, me and Justine , and the door opens, like the other nights when I drove up here.

Except this time, it's not a dude I don't know who opens the door. It's Big Head. He's still here. He doesn't look at us, he's staring behind us. I glance round, but can't see anyone. The street's well-lit, and it seems empty. As you'd expect, at one thirty in the morning in Kensington. It's not quite the same as the middle of Gloucester at this time. Justine goes past him and disappears through a door, clutching her wooden box.

Big Head signals at me to put the wine case on the hall table. I'm about to go and get the second wooden box, when he waves me further inside, and shuts the door. He's standing really close to me. 'Get back to Bristol now. You see someone following, you don' go back till you lose them. You understanding me, Joe?'

His voice sounds like he smokes those cigars for breakfast. He takes another breath and I can hear the faint wheezing; his lungs are not in good shape. The hard, dark eyes stare at me, and there's something in his look as he takes me in. Double chin bulging over the collar of his Armani shirt and tie, he breathes through his mouth, showing nicotine-stained teeth. I've never had a chance to take a good look at Big Head before, but now his face is so close to mine that a good look is what I'm getting, like it or not. And I don't like it. I don't like it at all.

Big Head's sweating, so much that now I can smell him. It's not Chanel. And I can hear him, I'm making the connection. I can hear that rasping breath. I can smell that smell. I'm back in the hospital, that endless night. Big Head is the Shadow on the Wall.

CHAPTER 9

Hell

I take a flying jump down all the steps, slam the boot, and hurl myself into the driving seat. Precious slips away through the quiet streets, staying on thirty; a cop car is the last thing I want behind me, now that I have a horrible idea what my real job description is.

There's nothing in my mirror except for an occasional taxi, as I head back towards the motorway. On the M4 there's just a procession of lorries cruising in the slow lane, and a few BMWs flying past.

I wish it was the middle of the rush hour. Then I wouldn't have time to think about all the other connections that are clicking into place like Lego. And the final link is in that wooden box. We're well clear of London as an exit junction looms into view. My throat is dry as I turn off, take a left at the roundabout, and drive a few miles before finding a lay-by to park in. It seems quiet enough. The headlights pick out an abandoned fridge and a pile of bin bags by the hedge, but I can't see anyone around. I open the boot. The second box looks just like the first, as I pull it towards me. It's sealed with small nails that are just tapped in.

I open the boot-well and take out the tool kit. It must be put there as a joke for dudes who buy Bentleys – they probably give it to the gardener to service the lawn tractor. I can't imagine your Bentley owner getting his hands messy to change a wheel, or even a light bulb.

A small wrench levers off the lid, and the boot lights gleam on a row of aluminium cigar cases lying in fake straw. I pull one open, and sniff. It smells of tobacco. But the box is deeper than where these cigars are.

There's a sudden rustling in the hedge. I stare around me, expecting to hear Big Head's wheezing breath in my ear. Nothing moves. My hands shake as I dig down into the fake straw, and find wood that moves slightly under my fingers.

The cigars and straw slide all over the boot, as I lift out the false floor. And I can see them now. They're each about the size of a singles pack of Revels, these small polythene bags with white powder in. Must be twenty of them, each one neatly sealed with a wire tag. I've never seen real cocaine before, but I've watched enough movies to know that this can't be anything else.

My mind is racing faster than this big powerful car ever could. With every delivery I do, I'm running Class A drugs under the cover of very expensive legal ones. DI Wellington's voice is in my head. 'Organisations like this never forget. They're a kind of Mafia… They could be looking for revenge.'

Big Head paid me that visit because they'd found out it was me who handed their driver to the police. Maybe he was planning to do more than just check me out. DI Wellington must have thought so when he brought in

Dave. But Big Head didn't get the chance that night; nor the night outside the cinema either.

So he reports back to Monsieur le Directeur, and they dream up a far more fun way of revenge. As if by magic – except there's no magic in this life, there are just plans that work or don't work – the ad appears on a website that I'm almost certain to find. Lenny tries to warn me off, because he knows about L'Étoile Fine Wines, and he's scared for me. Lenny's brother is in prison, and when you're locked up there I bet you find out about all kinds of things you didn't know before.

I must have given Monsieur such a buzz when I walked into that interview, just like a human target wandering into his gun sights. When I fell for everything – the car, the money, that blue-glass palace and the amazing glamour of it all. If Dad ever saw me now, I would want to die of shame. Monsieur is one of the criminals he's hunting. And I work for Monsieur. But if that's true, then something doesn't compute…

The corner of my eye catches a flicker behind me in the lanes. Headlights. And the drone of an engine. Seconds later Precious and I are rocketing through twists and turns. It's half one in the morning, and these narrow country roads are quiet, but I've never driven them before. Hedges jump up at me out of the dark as I swerve round sudden bends. The headlights are getting closer, blazing in my mirror. I have to turn, somewhere, and get back on the motorway.

There's a sign ahead – Waterhouse Farm? – and a track on the left. I clamp my foot hard on the brakes, praying that I won't have another rear end shunt, and swing up the tight entrance. The headlights veer on past. Precious bumps wildly through potholes as I stare ahead to see where I can turn.

Is that a farmyard on the right? We dive through the open gate into a yard surrounded by old stone barns, and suddenly we're in mud so deep and rutted it's like a ploughed field. I snap into reverse and those huge wheels spin, clumps of mud flying around us and spattering over the windscreen. For a split-second, I have a vision of me being towed out of here by the farmer's tractor. Or ducking, as he lines up his 12-bore because he thinks I've come to steal his cows in a Bentley.

Precious gets a grip, and we slither sideways out of the gate. The suspension crashes and bangs as I drive back down to the road, my hands greasy with sweat on the steering wheel. If Pursuit Car has found a place to turn, I've set the perfect trap for myself. There's no sign of headlights.

I blast back through the lanes, remembering the turns I took, in reverse order. Still nothing in my mirror. But I just know I'm going to see those headlights again. They're incredibly bright and blue, like Xenon types. So Big Head was right. I am being followed.

Then the thought explodes in my head, and I nearly drive into the ditch. Is it Big Head himself behind me? 'You see someone following, you don't go back till you lose them.' That would give him as many chances as he wants to finish me off and leave me by the roadside, pockets stuffed full of white powder to make it absolutely clear to my family, my friends and the police what I am.

I shove the accelerator and the lion growls. It's easy now getting back to the M4, there are signs at every junction. That makes it easy for Pursuit Car, too. He knows where I'm going, I'm sure of it. I join the M4 at Reading, and hit the Precious pedal harder than I've ever done. I know the Bentley Continental is the fastest saloon car around because Jeremy Clarkson says so. It can do two hundred and two mph, and that's what the speedo's saying now. But what's chasing me could be faster.

Twenty miles have flashed past when I see the glow of those Xenon headlights again. The beast behind me is very fast. Between us, we ought to be attracting some police attention. But there's not a blue light in sight. Then I remember where I can definitely attract some attention and get this dude off my back. We're heading for Swindon, home of speed cameras that actually work, and Very Efficient Cops.

At Junction 15 Precious sweeps up the slip road. We take a right, and enter these roadworks that are still there, more than a year after Grandad got papped. He was so annoyed with himself, doing forty two mph in the forty limit in return for three points on his licence. There's a left turn I can take to Highworth, just before a speed camera that will take a photo of Pursuit Car. IF I'm doing forty, and he isn't. If not, I'll get snapped first, and I don't need that.

We scorch along the single lane with cones either side. Just before each camera that flashes at everything doing more than forty, I slam on the brakes, and dude behind gets closer every time. Now I can see the sign, and there's the yellow camera. The needle's on eighty when I stamp on the brakes like I did on that test track, then yank the wheel hard left. The tyres scream as loud as any heavy metal gig. For one moment, I think we're going to become close friends with the hedge opposite. But the Bentley holds the line.

And Pursuit Car has no choice but to go straight on. I glance in my mirror as soon as we're through the turn. It's too late to see what's been following me, but there's a flash from the camera. I bet the driver's seen it. He knows that the Swindon police now have his number. I don't feel sorry for him.

A dull throb plays a drumbeat in my head as I drive back onto the M4. All I want to do is delete everything that's happened tonight, curl up in my big bed, and get on with my amazing new job tomorrow. As if.

Blue lights flash suddenly in my mirror, and my heart jumps. It's an ambulance, it passes, and I drive on, watching it disappear. I don't know how fast I dare go; there could be battalions of police chase cars out here now.

But the common sense part of my brain has switched to Survival mode. 'Look, Leah Wilks didn't give up, she came right back again. And so could this dude. Because he's faster than you. And it could be Big Head. He's in a different league from her.' Wearily, I agree with Survival Brain Department, come off the M4 at Bath, and set the sat nav for a B-road route back to Bristol. Takes two hours. But there are no more Xenon headlights behind me.

When I'm nearly in Bristol, the voice in my head gives me another prod, and I pull into a bus stop. White packets, fat cigars and fake straw are scattered all over the boot. Carefully, I put everything back where it was, and tap the lid down. I stare at that box. I wish I could chuck it into the ditch, and throw a grenade at it.

At half past four in the morning, I hit the remote, open the entrance doors and pull into the cave. As I slide out of the driver's seat, my legs feel like concrete. I take a look at Precious. In the half-light from the lamps on the cave walls, it looks more like a Land Rover, with its new mud-and-gold colour scheme. And I'm not like your usual Bentley chauffeur. Sweat is pouring off me, and I'm shaking with cold and hunger.

With a shock, I realize that a shadow with silver glistening hair has approached soundlessly, and is right beside me. 'This journey has taken you a long time, Joe.'

His voice is as quiet as ever, but I can hear a tension in it. Monsieur knew, just like Big Head, that I'd be followed. So there's no point in lying about that. I tell him everything about my trip back; except for the stop on the lay-by where I took a look at The Rest, and the next stop, where I tidied it up.

Monsieur's quiet for a few seconds. Then he says, 'There's a part of your story that is missing, Joe.'

I'm so horrified by the idea that somehow he knows I took a look in the boot, I can't think of anything to say. I just wait for him to give me the news about what happens now.

Monsieur walks round to the back of the Bentley, and passes his hand lightly across the rear screen. Some of the mud falls off, and in the dim lights of the cave I can see a small hole, towards the right hand side, with glass rippling away from it, in a kind of spider's web pattern. The hole is in line with the driver's head rest. It doesn't look like a stone's hit the rear screen. Whatever hit it was travelling way faster than a flying stone. My dull brain tells me that this was a bullet.

Maybe it was fired when the brakes were screaming so loudly in my sharp exit from the roadworks that I just never heard it. When Pursuit Car was so close, before I turned. I don't know. But the rear screen glass is as thick as the door window. It must have stopped that bullet, or at least slowed it down. Stopped it from going straight into the back of my head.

I can't see Monsieur's face in the shadows. His words come to me quietly out of the darkness, his voice sounding as grave as it did when he told me about the slaves. 'You did well to shake off that driver, Joe. You have brains, and you have courage. This is not the only time you will need both, while you work for L'Étoile Fine Wines.'

And in my bafflement and my rage, all I want to do is yell at him, 'You were on the same side as my dad, once! What turned you?'

CHAPTER 10

Mind Games

Hoping that the alarms haven't been set, I start to plod up the stairs to my flat, groping for the rail. A torch suddenly lights my way.

'You OK, son?'

I can just see the dim figure of the security guard. 'Yeah…'

'You look done in.' He walks behind me, shining his torch all the way up the stairs, and onto the lock of my apartment. The light guides the key in my unsteady hand.

'Thanks…'

'Look out for yourself.' He disappears into the darkness.

Without the energy even to grab a glass of water, let alone take off my sodden uniform, I crash onto my king-size bed. All the rest of the night, dreams blast through my head like bombs going off. I'm driving endlessly in the dark across muddy wastelands; gun fire rattles behind me, and headlights blaze brighter than the sun in my rear view mirror. Someone's sat beside me, but I can't tell if it's Dad or Monsieur. Once, when the car starts to skid towards a huge drop, my passenger grabs the steering wheel and pulls us back on course. And a voice in my head, like Dad's when I was with the Wilks woman, whispers 'You must drive faster, Joe.' So I do, and slowly those relentless headlights start to fade.

When I wake up, I'm parched and starving hungry, and my uniform's soaked with sweat. The alarm clock says eleven in the morning. I grab my mobile, and punch in DI Wellington's number. There's no signal. I roll off the bed and try the landline. It's dead.

My legs feel so heavy, it's like I'm waist-deep in water as I stumble down the back stairs to call with my mobile from outside. The door's locked, and I still don't have the key that Madame promised me.

Email! I force my legs to take the stairs back up four at a time. The chair wobbles as I crash onto it in front of the computer, and hit the keyboard with my password. No internet, just an error message.

I whack my hand onto the screen and get up, knocking over the chair. My head starts to throb again as I pace the room, and kick the fancy sofa with its stupid cushions. There's a soft thud on the window behind me. Thinking that a bird's hit the glass, I spin round, and see just bright blue sky.

Then, a small, twirling pink teddy pops up in front of me just outside the window, and plummets out of sight. I look down at the docks. And stare.

By the waterside, about ten people are grouped around Becks, looking on with interest as she whizzes the teddy round, about to chuck it again. She spots me, and starts jumping up and down, arms waving manically, one hand still clutching this pink teddy. The little gathering is a mixture of pensioners and Japanese tourists, and they look up at me as Becks does her windmill thing. I wave back at her, and point downwards. She runs off towards the side door.

The Japanese tourists clap appreciatively, and trot after her. They must think this is some kind of street theatre. Most of the pensioners wander back to their seats, shaking their heads, but two more hardy ones set off at a brisk walk after the Japanese dudes. I head back down the stairs.

Becks is tapping on the door. 'Joe, are you there?'

'Just HOW many people are listening in to us?'

She says to her audience, 'It's cool, thanks guys. I.. lost the keys to my apartment, and my mate's going to let me in now. Thanks… thank you… What?… Oh, you want to buy it as a souvenir? But there's loads of them in St Nicholas market, just up the road. I bought this one there, two pound fifty. Only, I had to stuff some stones into it, so it won't be quite the same…'

'Becks!'

'Let me get this straight. You'll give me ten pounds, if your friend takes a photo of me with teddy and you?'

'BECKS!!'

'I couldn't take ten. Make it five. Big smile!' Finally, she hisses through the door, 'It's OK, they've got their pic and wandered off.'

'Oh, right. You're sure they've not asked you to take them on a guided tour of the docks?'

'Stop wasting time, Joe! I couldn't get past Reception. They're not letting anyone in. Can't you open this door?'

'No chance.'

'Then, WHAT'S going on?'

'I don't know. I can't make any calls and my email's down. How come… ?'

'I worked all night and got my History coursework in a day early. I didn't like the way you sounded. Are you OK, Joe?'

I look behind me. Can't see anyone in the dark stairwell. But I remember how quietly Big Head's shadow slid into my hospital room. 'I've found out… something. It's not how I thought it was…'

'What d'you mean? What have you found out?'

The blackness in the stairwell seems to shudder slightly. 'Have to go. Listen up, Becks.'

'Joe! D'you want me to call DI Wellington?'

Her piercing whisper follows me past the twitching shadow, as I fly back up the stairs to my flat.

When I head into Reception five minutes later, I can't see Justine. The other movie star gives me a friendly smile.

'Hi Claire, is Justine around?'

Her phone rings, and she says as she picks up, 'No, lucky girl. She's off to Mauritius to top up her tan.'

I go into Madame's office. She looks up at me, taking in my crumpled uniform, as she taps away on her keyboard. Monsieur must have told her about last night.

'Is there a trip coming up soon, Madame?'

'Not at the moment, Joe, but there's never much warning, is there? There could still be a delivery tonight.'

'If I'm not needed right now, Madame, I'd like to go out and do some shopping?'

She stops tapping. 'Joe, Monsieur will tell you more soon, but we've had a bit of a security scare. None of our key staff are going out on the streets at the moment. If you need anything, just tell Claire, and she'll get it delivered.'

I wander back out into Reception and look at those glass doors. They can only be opened by a switch at the Reception desk. And there's a CCTV camera that films everyone going in and out. No quick exit there. But as I go back up the stairs, I have a plan. They can't block my calls when I'm on a delivery. I wait for the next shout, downing three bowlfuls of Cheerios to stop the hunger pains.

Eleven at night, and Madame hasn't called.

If this goes on, I can't get to the trial. It's only one week away now. I booked three days off for it. Now, I realize that Monsieur must know those are the dates when Leah Wilks is going into that courtroom. I've GOT to get out of here!

My soggy chauffeur's uniform makes my neck itch, as I try to think of my next plan. The itch turns into an idea. I tear off the uniform, change into jeans, and chuck it into the laundry trolley outside. Grabbing a load of towels from the bathroom, I climb inside the trolley and pull the whole lot on top of me.

It feels like hours later, and I'm almost suffocating with all this stuff on my head, when someone gives the trolley a shove. I'm pushed along miles of corridors, before we stop, and I hear a door hiss shut. We must be in the lift. My stomach somersaults as we go down, then jolt to a stand-still. The trolley's pushed along, then it stops again. Someone pulls all the towels and the uniform off me. Lights blaze into my eyes. And there is Monsieur.

What's weird is, he's not looking at me the way I thought he would. Not like I'm a rat in a trap that he's set for me. He looks at me like Mum and Grandad did, when I came home that night with a policeman at my side, and the policeman told them I was in big trouble. His voice sounds like theirs, too. It's worried. 'Come and sit down, Joe. We need to talk.'

We sit down in that huge room with the chandeliers. Monsieur rings through to Madame, 'No calls please, Françoise, until I say.'

Claire brings in a tray of coffee and biscuits. I try not to eat them all during the conversation that follows, but I'm so hungry there are no survivors.

When Claire's gone, Monsieur says quietly, 'The events of last night must have been terrifying for you, Joe.'

I open my mouth, then shut it again, as Survival Brain Department gives me a kick up the backside. One hint that I couldn't agree with him more, and I'll never leave this place alive. So I put on a broad grin. 'It was quite a buzz, really, like being in a Bond movie.' Then, I do aggrieved teenager. 'But tonight, I wanted to go clubbing, Monsieur. I've worked an awful lot of hours, but the door was locked, and Madame says no one's to go out at the moment. That's why I thought I'd try another way, that's all.' I give Monsieur a sheepish look, like, 'It's what teenagers do…'

'The reason the door was locked was because of a security alert, Joe. The phone system and email were also shut down, because we believe there is an organisation trying to hack into our IT network. We don't know yet who they are, or how dangerous they could be. We're protecting all our staff, including you, by keeping you here, until we know it's safe.'

He sounds like he's bought my story. But he's also made up one of his own. A security scare. What a great way of keeping people right where they are. Madame and the rest of the staff in this whole office block believe him, too. I can't resist testing Monsieur's knack for lying. 'The police will have the number of that car with the hit man in it that got snapped by the speed camera, Monsieur. So, are they onto him? Have they caught him yet?'

'That is not the kind of information that the police would give to anyone, Joe.'

He's right, of course. I feel a stab of anger. 'What about the Bentley? Have they been round to take a look at it?'

Monsieur looks at me steadily. 'The attempt on your life is a matter that I am handling personally, Joe. I know that I can be far more effective in dealing with it than the police.'

I stare at this man who I used to admire so much, and whose words I have no reason on earth to believe anymore. And I struggle with the idea that, somehow, I still want to trust him. Like I trusted him when we were tearing round that test track. I wish I could ask him about Dad. But Survival Brain Department says that could be a Really Bad Idea.

'So I… lie low for a bit, until you can send me out again, Monsieur? Is that the way it plays?'

'That's the way it plays, Joe. No clubbing for now.' Still he sounds Oscar-winning worried. Angry beyond words, I make my way back up to my flat and pace up and down.

Then, a thought strikes me. It's way past midnight, but Monsieur, Claire and probably Madame de L'Étang are still here, so the alarms can't have been set. This is my chance to do some night time reconnoitring. I check that my phone has plenty of battery to power the torch, stuff some cushions under the duvet in case someone checks up on me, switch off all the lights on my flat and creep down the stairs. Only the emergency lights are on here, with their dim green glow. As I get to the room with the chandeliers, a beam of light shines across the hall carpet from the door that's slightly ajar. Two men are talking in there. I can hear the quiet, iron-cold tones of Monsieur and Big Head's rasping voice. But they're talking in French. And if Monsieur isn't French, he's certainly an A★ linguist. Shaken, I try to make out some of the words. Big Head is muttering 'Tu sais bien que la choix n'est pas la tienne.'

Monsieur calmly replies, 'Non plus. C'est fini, Alfredo.'

'Espèce d'imbécile! Je peux faire ce que je veux, autrement tu sais bien ce qui arrivera…'

'Ton empire est foutu, c'est tout.'

Big Head's reply gets louder, and someone bangs the door shut with a force that makes me sprint down the next flight of stairs like a startled rabbit. In the empty reception area, I pause to get my breath and work out what I've heard. Monsieur was saying that something of Big Head's is finished, and Big Head wasn't taking too kindly to the idea. I'll have to think about it later. Right now I want to find out what else is in that underground car park apart from cars.

As I head down the stairs to the sous-sol, the air gets cooler. The silver XKR is still there but there's no sign of the yellow Lambo. Was that what it was behind me on the chase from London? The Lambo would certainly have the speed to catch the Bentley. Switching on my phone torch, I find the stairs to the cave below the sous-sol.

The air is as damp and cold as ever down here, with a smell of old wood and ancient stone. And there's the Bentley, gleaming softly in the torchlight. It's been cleaned up, but the bullet hole's still there. Remembering my first ever visit to this cave with Monsieur, I shine the torch over the rows of wine barrels that are nearly as tall as I am. Beyond the barrels, the racks of wine begin; there must be thousands of expensive bottles stored here, many of them coming in at the eye-watering cost of that 1995 Chateau Petrus. Monsieur said the temperature and atmosphere were ideal for storing fine wines. But what else are these dark, secret caverns ideal for storing?

I shine the torch beneath the wine racks. Nothing suspicious there. So I go back to the barrels, tap the first one with my torch and memorize the low thud it makes. The next one sounds the same as the first, and so do the rest. So either all the barrels are stuffed with cocaine, or all of them are full of wine, as wine barrels and cocaine barrels couldn't possibly sound the same.

Suddenly, another torch beam splits the darkness. Quickly, I switch mine off and slide behind the barrels. There's no mistaking this visitor, with that wheezing breath. I watch, knowing what the price of my curiosity could be, as Big Head crosses to the wall at the end of the cave. There's a rumbling, like a stone sliding aside, and he reaches inside some kind of hole in the wall. Before he even takes it out, I know that it's going to be one of those boxes that I found in the Bentley boot on that horrible night. A few minutes later, six boxes are stowed in the boot. Locking the car, he makes for the exit.

I creep out from behind the barrels and rack my brains to try and make sense of what I've seen and heard tonight. OK, Point One – I'm certain now that Monsieur really is French; he just speaks incredibly good English with barely a trace of an accent. But Point Two is far harder: if he's making all these pots of money selling fine wines, why on earth would he want to run drugs? And then there was that argument. Monsieur seemed to be defying Big Head, but Big Head was saying that Monsieur had no choice. If only I could talk to Becks; I know she'd figure it out in a flash.

I wait five minutes before tiptoeing back up the stairs to the sous-sol and then upwards towards my flat, holding my breath in case the alarms have been set and all hell's going to break loose. As I pass the room with the chandeliers, the light's still on. Suddenly I have such a strong urge to tell Monsieur everything, and get back to the trust we had in each other in the beginning. But Big Head could be behind that door. I go quietly on up to my flat. It's twenty past three in the morning. I set the alarm for seven thirty. Because I have one more plan ready to roll.

At nine in the morning, freshly showered, and stuffed with two bacon butties and a pint of coffee, I knock at the door of Madame's office. She looks tired, like she's been there all night, but her working hours are not top of my agenda. 'I do understand why I can't phone out of here, Madame. But I'm desperate to know about my Gran. She was taken into hospital two days ago to have a heart operation. And I would so like to know how she is.'

Madame frowns. 'I'm sure that your family can look out for her without you running the risk of making a telephone call, Joe. No one is accepting or making calls at the moment.'

I take a deep breath, and lie again. I am so good at lying now, I should get a certificate for it. What a shame they don't do it at GCSE. 'Madame, my grandmother lives in France. I just wanted to phone the hospital and ask after her.'

This puts Madame into deep thought. 'I will have to ask Monsieur le Directeur if this is possible, Joe. But I would be very surprised if he agrees.'

She calls up Monsieur, talking so quietly that I can't hear her, then puts the phone down, looking at me hard. 'For humanitarian reasons, Monsieur le Directeur says you may make this call. But it must be for no more than one minute.'

She hands me the phone. She can't see the keypad. So she can't see that I'm dialling the full international code for Britain, not France. To her, it looks like the right number of digits. It is. But I'm dialling Becks' landline. Praying that she'll be there, that she can read my mind. Because this is my last chance.

The phone rings, and the clock's ticking. Sixty, fifty-nine, fifty-eight... Someone picks up, I hear the click that says Monsieur is listening in, and I babble, calling up all my GCSE French, 'Je voudrais parler avec le médecin qui soigne ma grandmère, s'il vous plait. Je m'appelle Joseph, je suis son grandfils. C'est très urgent.'

There's an intake of breath on the end of the line. It's Becks' breath, I'm sure it is. 'C'est très urgent, s'il vous plait.' Please let her recognize my voice!

Becks could blaze a career in Hollywood. She puts on an official kind of voice, and says with a brilliant French accent, 'Et bien, Monsieur, et le nom de votre grandmère?'

'Elle s'appelle Annette, Mademoiselle.' The name of Steve's French girlfriend should convince Becks that it's me calling, not some crazy hoaxer.

I look at Madame's face, staring at me hard across her desk, and it's a blank. Now I know she can't speak French. But can Becks and I outsmart Monsieur le Directeur? All bets are still on. Thirty, twenty-nine, twenty-eight…

Becks is trying to work out a code to reply to my message. 'Vous voudriez savoir si tout va bien avec votre grandmère, Monsieur?'

'Oui Mademoiselle, c'est très important.'

'Je peux vous informer que tout va bien avec votre grandmère, Monsieur.' Then she says, 'Est-ce que vous avez un message pour votre grandmère, Monsieur?'

Eighteen, seventeen, sixteen… What message, what cry for help, can I send Becks without giving the game away, before Monsieur susses us and cuts me off? I'm racking my brains, when Commander Julius Grayling's familiar voice whispers in my mind. 'Il faut prier,

Mademoiselle. On a besoin de prier.' Becks knows I'm not asking for prayers for my imaginary French grandmother. She knows that I'm the one who needs them.

Five, four, three… 'Merci Mademoiselle, c'est tout. Aurevoir.' Before Madame can take the phone away from me, I put it down.

Madame says, like her teeth are clamped together, 'I had no idea that you could speak French so well, Joe. And how is your grandmother? Is she doing well after the operation?'

'They say my Gran's OK. But she's eighty-two, so…'

The phone rings. It won't have taken Monsieur any time at all to trace the number I dialled, and find out that it wasn't a French hospital. That it wasn't France at all.

Madame listens, nods and says 'Of course. Yes, straightaway.' It has to be Monsieur. He must be pretty annoyed now, and not for humanitarian reasons.

Madame puts the phone down, and looks up at me with her dark beady eyes. 'It appears that we have a trip for you after all, Joe. You will be down in the carpark with the Bentley in five minutes. There is a consignment that needs urgent delivery.'

As I button the jacket of my chauffeur's uniform, I know that this is the last time I'll ever do it. Three minutes later, I'm in the cave. Someone's standing in the shadows near the Bentley. But there's no glittering silver hair. Instead, a torch shines right into my eyes. 'Get in the car, Joe.'

I don't move. Big Head's sixty cigars-a-day voice says again, 'Get in the car.'

'I have a question to ask Monsieur.'

'You don' ask questions, Joe. Get in the car.'

I still don't move. 'Why did Monsieur give me this job?'

Big Head likes this. He chuckles chestily before replying, with a directness that convinces me this is my last trip, 'You mess up his plans, Joe. The woman who is ours, you hand to the men in suits. You give them information. So, we bring you here. Easy. How you fall for that ad, don' you? Fast car, beautiful girls, good money. All you wan', isn't it, Joe?'

'You're just a bunch of dirty drug runners!'

'You too, Joe. Part of the firm now. Get in.'

I've had it being pushed around by Big Head. 'You've no idea how much information the police already have about you, do you? For all you know, this trip could be your biggest ever mistake.'

That rattles his cage. 'Shut up! You go to Birmingham. Drop the goods, come back with a passenger. You don' talk to her. You don' call any of your friends in suits. You understanding me, Joe? Because you better be understanding me.' He takes another rasping breath. 'Or something happens to your family...'

And I was feeling so clever.

Big Head says, 'Take a look.' His voice hardens. 'Not holiday photos.' He holds up his phone. He watches me, enjoying himself, as I look at the tiny screen. I can see my house. The camera pans across the windows, the front door, and I can see Mum's Citroën on the driveway. The lens moves slowly round the inside of another car, and onto the front passenger seat. Lying there as casually as a handbag is a black 9 mm revolver.

Big Head snaps shut the phone. 'Address is on the sat nav. You been there before. Get in, Joe.'

Feeling numb, I do what he says.

'You're not there in ninety minutes, your family has visitors. And we call the police. We tell them there's a Bentley, two kilos of cocaine in the boot, on the way to a drop.'

Big Head's mouth is close to my ear, and I can smell his stinking breath again. 'You call anyone, we see you an' we hear you. You wan' see your people again, Joe, you don' mess up.'

—⁂—

The sun blasts straight into my eyes, as I drive out of the cave for the last time. I don't need the sat nav to tell me who I'm collecting. I remember DI Wellington: 'she's attracted so much police attention, she'll be no more use now to whoever's employing her.'

I take quick glances around me as I head up the M5. The Bentley's stuffed with tiny cameras and microphones. There's one behind the rear view mirror, and others concealed in the interior lights. They were always there; I just didn't see them. No reason to suspect anything when you're in heaven.

There must be more cameras in the boot. Monsieur knew the moment I wrenched open that wooden box that I'd recognized Big Head.

Now Big Head's sending me on my final drop. And his plan is neither me nor Leah Wilks is ever going to get to that courtroom. One way is, we'll be shot by whoever put the bullet into the Bentley – maybe Big Head himself.

The other way is, we have blue lights flashing, and I get arrested and locked up for a long time, for driving hundreds of kilos of Class A all over the UK. Just like Jamie.

On balance, I think that's better than being gunned down. Unless Big Head tells the police, in his public-spirited, anonymous tip-off, that we're armed, and my passenger is a crack shot with a Magnum. That way, we also end up dead.

I know Becks will have got onto DI Wellington. But what can he do when he doesn't know where I am? And I have no way of telling him, with those Big Brother mics and cameras. If I even try I'll just put my family in more danger.

I remember one of my English lessons where Mr Russell, the only teacher I really rated, asked me to give an example of Being Between A Rock And A Hard Place. I thought I did quite well at the time. I said: 'There's a gig with the Red Hot Chillies I've been given a ticket to, then my best mate invites me to his 16th on the same night, and there's going to be free food, and gorgeous girls.'

Right now, I'd give that answer a U. The A* answer is: 'You're a known drug runner, you have a boot full of cocaine, and you can get shot by a drugs gang or you can get shot by the police. Which way do you want it?'

I wonder what Commander Julius Grayling would do.

CHAPTER 11

End Game

Silently, Precious glides to a halt outside the Birmingham house where Leah Wilks has gone into hiding. It's a fine place to make the last delivery of my glittering career as a drug runner. If anything, it looks slightly tackier than when I drove Big Head up here a couple of days ago. A bin bag lolls on the pavement, spewing empty baked bean cans and cider bottles from a rip in the side. Next to the battered front door a cracked window pane is propped up against the wall. An old Ford Sierra is parked outside, its rear window smashed; shards of glass sparkling in the road. No sign of any kids puffing on fags this time.

I get one of the boxes out of the boot and lock the Bentley. When I turn back to the house, Leah Wilks is standing in the doorway. She looks about as friendly as she did at our first meeting. 'I can't believe Alfredo Bertolini said it would be you, shitface.'

She must mean Big Head. 'He also said we're not to talk.' I jump, as a man suddenly appears behind her in the dark hallway. His sallow face has a week's growth of beard. The baggy jeans are scarred with burn marks. Small, bloodshot eyes squint at me as he pushes past her, taking in my uniform. 'They said they'd send a driver, not a blasted cop!'

I hold out the box. 'Cops don't do door-to-door.'

'Oh, we've got a clever one, 'ave we?' He grabs it from me.

'The next delivery's running late.' I turn, but Leah Wilks isn't there. Then I see her, standing by the Bentley. She actually wants to go on this journey. What the hell has Big Head told her?

I press the remote to unlock the doors. She gets inside and sits staring straight in front of her. The man glares at her contemptuously. 'Stupid cow.' He goes back inside with the box, kicking the door shut behind him.

I dart nervous glances sideways as Precious floats quietly through the streets. Wilks is ominously quiet. Just behind us, a truck gives a blast like a ship's fog horn. She never twitches. I wonder how on earth I'm going to get through to her without igniting that deadly violence. But before I can even try, I've got to do something about the eyes and ears that are picking up my every move. I drive slowly for a couple of miles, pull into a side street and stop.

'What's the game?'

'There's something wrong with the gearbox. I can't go any faster than 20. I'll have to take a look at the fuses.'

'You better not try anything…'

'If I don't fix this, we're not going to Bristol.' I get out, and reach into the footwell for the fuse box lid. There must be fifty or more fuses, each with a coded label. I had to replace a bulb once and it took half an hour with the handbook before I finally found BLN, for

Brake Light Nearside. So where's the code that will let me knock out those mics and cameras? Sweat trickles down my face. I take off the stupid chauffeur's cap and slip it inside the car. Slow movements. Nothing that'll wind her up.

The maze of codes stares at me. HLO; Headlamp Offside. RU; Refrigeration Unit. ICES; In-Car Entertainment System. My heart thuds as I imagine the gunman outside my house, waiting for the call. Thirty miles away from him, Big Head watches Leah Wilks, frozen in the passenger seat. Inside a Bentley that's going nowhere. Nervously, I feed the mics. 'I think I've found the right fuse... at least, I hope I have'.

Then I see it – CCTVS. Computer Controlled Traitor Vision System? Or Closed Circuit Television System? I yank the fuse out. The green lights that said On have gone off. Now I wonder if the engine's going to start, as I might also have pulled the plug on Car Control That's Very Secret. But the lion growls again.

Her voice is quiet. 'OK, toe rag, stop once more and you'll get a taste of the same medicine you got last time.'

I daren't try and talk to her yet. I head for the M5. Racking my brains for a way of convincing her that this man she seems to trust wants to kill us both. Praying that he'll think I pulled out that fuse by accident. I'm still out of ideas as we approach the Worcester junction. The weather's changing. The sun's gone in, and dark clouds are ballooning up from the horizon. More and more cars pour onto the motorway.

I take a deep breath, trying to keep my voice matter of fact. 'Alfredo said we can talk... once we're out of Birmingham.'

'Shut up an' drive.'

Massive black clouds are taking over the sky. Heavy rain is falling up ahead. And now I can see the car behind us, closing so fast. It's a Jag XKR, silver-coloured, like the one in the basement. It could be any silver XKR, just trying for a burn-up with a Bentley. But I can't risk it. I floor the accelerator. Precious sounds interested; I can hear the deeper breaths go into the engine. We're on a run.

'What you playin' at?'

'I think someone's after us.'

Her eyes flick to the passenger door mirror. 'Which car?'

'The Jag.'

She stares into the door mirror. 'Why?'

'They don't want us to get to Bristol.'

'Then bloody drive faster!'

Like I'm not trying to. I'm doing 100 whenever I can but the XKR's gaining on us. There's so much traffic, my brain's working like a supercomputer. Then my eye's caught by a flashing light, up near the clouds. My hands tighten on the wheel. I don't know if it's police, but it's definitely a copter.

I glance back into my mirror, and go cold. The XKR's around a hundred yards behind us. There's an arm outside the passenger window, and a gun that's aimed right at us. I rocket across the motorway, carving up a totally innocent white van, and we drive into darkness.

The rain comes down like a car wash at full bore. I switch on the headlights and slow down. Anything over fifty would be insane, even with the awesome grip of those huge tyres. The wipers are on double speed, but

I can still hardly see. It's impossible to make out what's behind us.

All the traffic's piling up, brake lights blazing out red warnings right up the motorway. We're almost at the Evesham junction, still in the slow lane after my dive away from Hitman. The torrential rain is being swept off the windscreen in bucket loads by the thrashing wipers, as I turn off the M5. A queue of cars follows us, but I can't see if the XKR is among them. I drive a couple of miles towards Evesham, then slip into a lay-by. There's no one behind us.

'You got it coming now, shitface.'

'There's something you need to see.'

The storm's easing a bit, but the rain soaks us in seconds as we get out. I push the water away from the bullet hole, remembering Monsieur lightly brushing off the mud that night. Then, I stare at the second bullet hole, inches away from it. Tiny pieces of glass on the rear parcel shelf flash in the headlights of passing traffic.

Leah Wilks reaches out and runs a finger over the two spider's webs. 'So, they shot at us. That what you're crappin' yourself about?'

My brain's doing a thousand miles an hour. 'Alfredo said this could happen. He told me what we have to do.'

Quick as a flash, she's got me in a headlock so tight I can hardly breathe. 'Listen to me, scum. I'm the one Alfredo talks to. 'E told me the only way he can get the police off my back is if we stay on the M5 all the way to Bristol. So move your arse!'

The rain's just drizzle now. A pale sun peers through the clouds, a beam catching the rich wood of the dashboard. I stare at the water trickling down the windscreen. Big Head's end game is way cleverer than I thought. If his hitman didn't score first time he knew I'd get off the motorway. So he made absolutely certain that Wilks was onside, to give his gunman a second chance. She thinks Big Head is God. I'll never persuade her to go with me to the police now.

I shift into Drive, and head back to the M5, watching her out of the corner of my eye. She seems more relaxed, now that I'm doing what Alfredo says. Flicking open her window, she lights a cigarette.

The closer we get to the M5, the more my brain dodges and weaves, trying to think of a way out of this. We approach the last roundabout before Junction 9, where I gave the XKR the slip. Half of my brain is still on Get Out, and half is on the truck that's far too close behind me. There's a petrol station at the second exit of the roundabout. I glance at the fuel level. Quarter of a tank. Plenty to get us to Bristol. If we ever make it down the M5. I indicate right, and slow down to give way to a massive camper van. It trundles past, and Precious swings onto the roundabout. As I check in the passenger door mirror, it explodes.

My foot hits Kickdown so hard we leave a burst of tyre smoke behind us. The screaming wheels power through the roundabout, and back onto the road we've just travelled. I keep my foot clamped to the floor, overtaking cars, coaches, trucks, the second there's a gap. Ten miles on, the breath rattles in my throat, as I ease off behind the artic in front.

I risk a glance at Leah Wilks. In a daze, she stares at the tiny shards of mirror glass that sparkle all over her black tracksuit. She tries to brush them off. Then she shudders, as a drop of blood trickles from her right thumb. A piece of glass about the size of a pin is sticking out of it. She stares at the thumb like it's being sawn off in front of her. Then, her face grey, she starts to retch. She can't take the sight of her own blood. I pull quickly into the next lay-by. She stumbles out of the Bentley. As I reach for my phone, I can see her throwing up into the hedge.

'Joe, at last!'

'My family?'

'All fine, Joe. Rebecca got straight onto us after your call. The gunman outside your house is now our guest.'

'Becks? They'll know her number now…'

'She's here with us. We've got an armed car near the house. Now where are you?'

'Four miles from the M5 Junction 9. We've been shot at, twice.'

'Is the Wilks woman with you in the car?'

'She'll be back any time. Something came up.'

'Be very careful, Joe. Don't try any heroics.'

'I'm not sure I know what heroics are, Inspector.'

He draws in his breath. 'The copter's on the case again now they can see, but they haven't found you yet. Now listen, Joe…'

Twenty seconds later, I stuff the phone out of sight, as Leah Wilks gets slowly back into the car. I say quickly, 'It's OK. We're going on down the M5. Like Alfredo said.' I turn back towards Junction 9. DIW's sending a car to that petrol station. But the XKR won't be there anymore. It'll be waiting for us, somewhere out on the motorway. Slowly, I reach out my hand, and flick the switch to close Wilks's window.

As we accelerate down the slip road, another raging storm of clouds floods across the sky. It's as black as night. I give the pedal a giant shove. The lion bellows back to me, as the Bentley takes a spine-busting leap forwards, soaring to 180 with its massive, sweet music.

Twenty miles to Michael Wood services. I stamp on the throttle again. The Ferrari in front scoots out of the way like we're scorching his tail. The Bentley's powerful headlights are blazing the trail up to a mile ahead, when suddenly I see twinkling helicopter lights above us again. Leah Wilks sees them too. 'Is that police?' The voice has an edginess to it.

The Cheltenham turn-off flashes into view, and disappears into the dark like it was never there. If she tries to break my arm again, we'll crash at two hundred miles an hour. The end will be so quick, neither of us will ever know about it. Nothing can save you at less than half this speed. Not even Precious. At least there's no one around to take with us.

I try to keep my voice calm. 'It's Alfredo's copter. Remember what he said? He's going to make sure you get to Bristol.'

''E never told me 'e had a copter.' I can hear a trace of resentment. Suspicion.

'He only uses it to look after his favourite drivers. You must be one of them. I know I'm not.'

The flattery works, too well. Now, she's looking up at that copter like it's her VIP escort. I wish she wouldn't. Because it's going to drop down from the sky long before Bristol.

The motorway's almost empty as we tear past the Gloucester exit. Just beyond, there's a wide area on the hard shoulder. I usually slow down here. Quite often, there's a cop car with some motorist who's been pulled over. But the car there isn't police. As we fly past, the Bentley's headlights gleam on the silver metal of a long cigar shape. Looking back, I see its lights snap on.

At first we lose the XKR completely. The mirror's dark. Then, there's a faint glow, maybe two miles behind. This is no ordinary XKR. It must be doing 250 to catch up so quickly. It'll be on us well before we get to Michael Wood. I move into the fast lane. 'Get down on the floor.'

Her voice is as tight as a wire. 'What are you up to now?'

'See those lights in the mirror? It's the Jag again.'

'But Alfredo's copter…'

'The copter can't stop the Jag shooting at us again. Now get down. Or you'll get it in the head, like you nearly did last time.'

She's seen the lights closing on us. Wordlessly, she slides onto the floor and crouches, her hands gripping the seat as we rocket onwards. The glow turns into a blaze of headlights. I haven't the brains to work out how close the XKR needs to get before we take another bullet. My foot hits the Precious brakes, harder than ever before. We go from two hundred to twenty in a few rib-tearing seconds. Wilks' knuckles are white as the huge deceleration drags her into the footwell. Her nails rip into the leather seat.

There's a scream of tyres behind us, and lights fill the mirror. I brace myself for another shunt. Then the XKR swerves around us, still braking hard. It's ahead of us now on our left, in the middle lane. That gun pointing out of the passenger window can't fire at us yet.

I pull alongside the Jag, and swing the wheel hard left. Precious slams into those sleek silver panels. Metal clashes against metal, again and again, as I keep on shoving the XKR towards the hard shoulder. A few feet to my left the driver's hands flail around on the steering wheel. I can't see his face. Keeping level, I swing the wheel again. Another sideways collision, and he's on the hard shoulder. I give him another shove. Mustn't let him get control back.

Suddenly, the gun barrel is aiming right across the driver's face, at me. A dull thud paints another spider's web, in Wilks's inch thick window this time. Furiously, I swing the Bentley out then charge back at the weaving XKR. There's a long graunch of tearing metal as I keep contact. Braking, because the Jag's slowing. I think only two wheels are on the ground now, but I have to make sure. I take another sideways smash at it and now I can see its underside, wheels in the air.

The XKR rolls over in slow motion. Then it crashes onto its roof, slides a few yards with a scream of metal, and stops, like a giant upside down beetle that can't fly anymore.

My whole body's shaking and sweating as I ram the accelerator to the floor. Headlights blazing skywards, the wreck disappears from my mirror into the dark. We're back in the fast lane doing two hundred again. I wipe the sweat out of my eyes, and stare ahead at the sign. Two miles to Michael Wood. There's a movement to my left, as Wilks slips back into the passenger seat. I hear the click of her seatbelt.

Seconds later, the turn off hatches flash into view. I leave it right to the last nanosecond before changing course. We zap across the lanes and Monsieur's beautiful, battle-scarred Bentley swoops off the motorway like a Lear jet coming in to land. I jam on the brakes. It's as though we've got parachutes behind us. Not a chirp from those fat tyres.

We're down from two hundred mph to around ten. Three chase cars wait, blue lights flashing, headlights blazing. The copter hovers at around sixty feet, rotors thundering like machine gun fire. Armed police run towards us.

'Bastard!' Leah Wilks' hands are round my throat. I can't breathe. The pain rips down my spine and up into my head. She's going to break my neck. The darkness comes down. I can feel the Bentley veering wildly, as my foot fights to stay on the brake pedal.

Someone tears open my door, grabs the steering wheel and stops the engine. Those deadly hands are pulled from my neck. A voice says, 'You really shouldn't have done that.'

At first, I think he's talking to me. There are so many things I really shouldn't have done. Then, I've got air again, and I can see. She fights like a wildcat, as three cops struggle to drag her away.

'No time to waste, Joe!' DI Wellington rushes me into the back of a Vauxhall Omega, yelling, 'Go!'

The car takes off like the start of a Formula One. I slide back in the seat, part of my brain expecting the click of handcuffs round my wrists any time. But an iron grip clasps my hand, and a familiar face grins at me. Robocop Dave says, 'Been getting around a bit, haven't you, mate?'

—⁓—

As we pull up outside my house, there's a dull weight in my stomach. In spite of all Dave's light-hearted banter, this still feels so much like that first night when I came home in a police car.

Dave looks at me as his hand goes up to the doorbell. 'You alright, Joe?'

'Yeah…'

'Lighten up, mate. Your mum's just glad you're in one piece.' He pushes the bell, then gives me a whack on the back that would deck a horse. 'And, off the record, you could give our chase drivers a lesson or two, know that?'

I'm still reeling when the door opens, and Mum's stood there. She looks at me for a second, up and down, like she wants to make sure it really is me. Her eyes are bright, but her hair looks as if she's not washed it in a week.

'I'm sorry, Mum.' The words come out in a croak, like my voice hasn't broken yet. She takes a little step forwards on tiptoes, and her arms reach up and go tightly round me. I hug her back. She feels so small. How was she ever strong enough to carry me around when I was a kid?

'You didn't know what you'd got mixed up with, love. God knows how you got out of it alive. Your grandad and I think you're incredibly brave!'

'I... what?'

Grandad appears in the doorway. He's got a sticking plaster on his chin, and half of his face is shaved while the other half is all bristly. He clears his throat awkwardly, and puts on a frown. 'Are you two going to stand outside all night?' He turns to Dave. 'Thank you for bringing him home safe, Officer. Would you like a cup of tea?'

'Thanks, but I'll be getting on. Still got two hours shift.' Dave jams his police cap back on his head. It reminds me of my chauffeur headgear that I must have left in the Bentley. He slaps my back again, not quite so hard this time. 'You take care now, mate. And your people are right – you did OK.'

As Dave's car pulls away into the night, Jack belts down the stairs. 'Hey, Joe, guess what! Those cop cars've got panels that drop down from the doors when they open. Stops the hit man shooting at their legs!'

Mum explodes. 'Jack! The police told you to keep away from the windows while that horrible man was out there!'

Grandad says wearily, 'Let's all have a cup of tea. Then can we please go to bed?'

—◊—

My room looks so cosy after that big, lonely apartment. Fats is curled up on my pillow like a black and white furry cushion. I run my hand over his smooth coat. He opens amber eyes and yawns, showing his small pink tongue, then tucks his head back into his paws.

Jack pops his head round the door. His hair's growing back so fast from the crew cut, he looks like a hedgehog. 'Did you actually get shot at on the motorway, Joe? Mum and Grandad were just whispering into the phone when the police dude called… I couldn't catch all of it.'

'I got shot at. How are the angel fish? Still making a meal of their kids?'

'The female died.'

'Oh crap!'

He shrugs. 'It was fungus, not grief for the eggs the male ate. And she was quite old, for an angel. We gave her a good funeral in the garden. Night, Joe.'

As the door closes behind Jack, I take the photo of Dad out of my drawer. 'What would you make of all those wicked people, Dad?' And that ache comes back so badly that I have to sit down on my bed, my head in my hands, just gazing at his laughing blue eyes. There's a light tap on my door. 'Joe, are you still awake?'

'Come in, Mum.'

She's wrapped in her dark blue dressing gown, carrying an envelope. 'I found this while I was sorting through your father's photos, Joe. And I thought that, given the extraordinary qualities you seem to have inherited from him, you should have the last letter he wrote to me.' She holds it out and I take it slowly.

'Didn't he use email?'

'It would have been intercepted. Ironic, isn't it? The only secure way was for him to post a hand-

124

written letter while he was on leave, hoping that he wasn't being tailed.'

'Thanks, Mum.'

'Night, sweetheart.' She takes my face gently in her hands and lightly kisses the top of my head, then her dressing gown rustles through the door and she's gone.

The ink on the letter is a faded black, but I can still read the strong, dramatic brush strokes of my father's handwriting. I reckon, if he'd been able to email this letter, he'd have used Broadway. Fats climbs cautiously onto my lap, and I rest my hand on his soft coat as I read.

Chérie

I miss you and the boys desperately, and hope that you are all well. I am in a place which you and I visited on our honeymoon – tu te rappelles a certain casino? I am here with a colleague taking some leave from the demands of investigating my current target, with whom I have succeeded in getting myself hired as bodyguard. How I wish I could come home for a few days to see you all, but sadly that is impossible as I would inevitably be followed. My new employer is as suspicious as she is dangerous.

This is a dark place where I work. Life is held cheap, and it makes me angry to see how callously these powerful men and women dispose of those who are no longer of any use to them. But I remain hopeful that I and my trusted colleagues around the world are doing a job that even the SAS, my erstwhile employer, could not. We are so deeply embedded with the enemy that they see us as their own. Building that trust is part of our job, so that they come to divulge more and more information. And when the time is right, we make our move to bring them down.

Cherie, you must not worry about my safety. I know what I am about, and I have the support of my magnificent colleagues whom I trust with my life. Our motto is that of the legendary musketeers – 'Tous pour un, un pour tous'. This is a worthy enterprise that we are engaged in and one day, when I am back home at last and can tell the whole story, I want you and the boys to be as proud of me as I am of you all.

Tell our splendid boys that their father thinks of them always, and give them a huge hug from me. Quant à toi, ma belle Nina, je t'embrasse comme toujours.

Ton
Julius

Fats nudges the letter with his nose as I sit with it in my hands, motionless. The voice of the man who wrote it is so like the voice that whispered in my head, out there on the M5, that it's uncanny. Carefully, I fold the letter around Dad's photo and place them in my drawer. I know there will be many times when I'll need to look at them again. But at least now I have something more to find comfort in. It must have cost Mum a lot to part with this keepsake.

As I close the drawer, tiredness hits me like a tsunami. My uniform feels glued to me as I peel it off. It's like shedding a skin. Wriggling under my duvet, I'm not sure if I want to turn off the light. Will there be more gun shots, as soon as I close my eyes? Then I think, well it wouldn't bother Commander Julius Grayling. Fats purrs loudly in my ear, and puts a big soft paw on my face. I reach out my hand, click off the bedside lamp, and sleep without the shadow of a dream. Only that peaceful rumbling in my head.

—⁓—

'Detective Inspector Wellington said we're all to carry on as normal. Not let this take over our lives. Just keep an eye open.' Mum puts a cup of coffee in front of me as we sit at the breakfast bar in the kitchen. Her hair looks all fluffed out, like she's had a shower and dried it carefully. Grandad's sorted the shaving situation, so now both sides of his face look symmetrical, including the two sticking plasters.

It's a Sunday, thankfully. I'd lost all track of time. We all slept in until midday, and my stomach's gurgling happily after its reunion with Mum's bacon and eggs. I flick cautious glances at her and Grandad. 'Is it OK if I go out, then?'

Jack shovels baked beans on toast into his mouth and mumbles, 'Watch out for the shooters!'

Mum pauses as she refills the kettle. 'WHAT did you say, Jack?'

'Scooters… Joe's been on the internet, watching out for a scooter. Haven't you, Joe?'

'Yeah…' I take a swig of coffee, and glare at Jack.

'Where are you off to, Joe?' Grandad spreads butter onto his toast and reaches for the marmalade, his eyes catching mine almost accidentally.

'Just a meet with Becks in Stroud. We thought we'd take in a film, then go for a pizza?'

He fishes in his pocket and pushes a couple of notes towards me. 'Have it on us. But mind how you go.'

'Cheers, Grandad.' I can't meet his eyes, and my face is burning as I close the front door behind me. I think, 'I worry so much, about you worrying about me.' Then the bus trundles round the corner, and I sprint to catch it. Looking down from the top deck, I'm amazed at how small and pretty the streets of Stroud are, after the wide roads of Bristol with their huge office blocks. Maybe Becks and I will just go and see a film after all, then catch up over a pizza.

She meets me at the bus station. Her mane of red hair is pulled sleekly back into some kind of tuft with beads in it. 'God, Joe, you look awful.'

'Thanks. You look great.'

'No, I mean… you've got these big bags under your eyes, and you must have dropped at least two kilos. Come on – BK.' She grabs my hand.

'Too pricey. But there's some great burger deals going at the new cafe by the station.'

'By the station…' The green eyes look at me, quad core brain on the case.

Twenty minutes later, she stares at my empty plate while I check out the menu. 'You didn't tell me you've only just had breakfast. You can't possibly eat another one – you'll be ILL!'

'Watch me.'

'No thanks!'

'Sure you don't want another?'

She takes the menu off me. 'I could maybe just manage a choc sundae.'

As I join the queue, I notice the big, black-haired guy at the front of it, and my stomach does a flip. He's got sticking out ears, and he's in a dark coat. My heart starts to thump, and I strain to hear his voice as he gives the cashier his order. Then, the woman next to him nudges his arm. She points at a poster on the wall, with a mega whoppa, gut-busting, cholesterol-boosting meal deal. He turns to look, and it's not Big Head. But by the time I get back to Becks, my appetite's blown to pieces. I just stare at the burger.

'You alright?'

'Eyes too big, that's all.'

'Told you.' Becks digs deep into the choc sundae, then pauses, the loaded spoon in mid-air, her eyes thoughtful. 'D'you think they'll get him?'

'Who – Bertolini or Monsieur?'

'Bertolini?'

I look around for the dude with sticking out ears. He must have left the cafe. But I still whisper. 'I think Alfredo Bertolini is Big Head's real name.'

'And he was the one who was shooting at you?' The spoon-load disappears into Becks' mouth.

'Not so loud! I don't know. I couldn't see the face behind the gun. And Dave said the XKR was empty when they found it.'

'But it was Big Head who sent you on that run. It had to be him, didn't it? He didn't want you and that woman to get to the trial.'

'That was what it looked like.'

'What are you saying, Joe?'

'I'm saying I just don't know who's the boss. It could have been Monsieur who gave the orders for that pick up.'

Becks' spoon probes into the sundae for bits of chocolate. 'Monsieur doesn't seem… dangerous… does he?'

'DIW must think Monsieur's dangerous. Otherwise he wouldn't have sent in armed cops to raid the offices as soon as he got your call.'

She looks up from the sundae, and I get 1000 watts of green eyes. 'What do YOU think, Joe? About Monsieur?'

'I don't know what to think, Becks. Not anymore. I'm sure he knew what was in the boot. And he didn't seem surprised that someone had taken a shot at me that night. He just didn't look too happy about it.'

She says softly, 'The boss was well OK at first, wasn't he? It was your dream job.'

'Dream job for a loser.'

'Stop feeling sorry for yourself and concentrate! Do you really think it could have been Monsieur who sent that hitman after you? And planted the gunman outside your house?'

'I don't want to think so. But I have to know.'

'OK. And that's why we're eating here, isn't it? Next to the station?'

The train bowls in, we find an empty carriage, and Becks curls up comfortably on the seat opposite. It's a bit annoying that she doesn't look the tiniest bit surprised; she could earn a stack as a mind reader.

'You think Monsieur is still in the building, don't you?'

'It's just a feeling…'

'So, why don't you tell the police, and let them find him?'

'I don't want them to find him. Not yet, anyway. I HAVE to ask him…'

'If he's the boss who ordered the shootings? D'you think he'd tell you? He's got half the police on the planet after him – he must have other things on his mind than a cosy chat with you.'

'It's more than that, Becks, don't you see? If he's not the boss, he could end up in prison for stuff that's nothing to do with him.'

'Nothing to do with? You were driving his car all over the country with bootloads of Class A!'

'That doesn't mean it was him giving the orders.'

Becks pushes a dark red curl behind her ear, like she does when she's in the middle of an Eng Lit essay. 'Are you saying you think this Tortellini…'

'Bertolini.'

'Canelloni, whatever. You think he's the real boss?'

'I… well…' I fish in my pocket for my pack of Revels. A small black stick like an iPod comes out with the chocs, and falls on the carriage floor.

Becks retrieves it. 'What is it?'

'The remote for the basement carpark. I found it when I was getting out of my uniform last night.'

She takes the pack of Revels, pours herself a handful before chucking it back to me and says, through a mouthful of chocolate, 'Sweet.'

CHAPTER 12

The Slave Trail

Blue lights are flashing all around the main reception of the Fine Wines tower block when we arrive. We retreat into an alley, and take the back route to the basement entrance, keeping close to the wall. The sliding doors are closed. There's an armed cop standing right outside.

Becks whispers, 'Stay out of sight!' She breaks into a run and dashes up to him. 'Please! You've got to DO something!' I have to admire the half-sob in her voice.

He swings round, his hand going to his holster. 'What's up?'

'I was just coming out of the multi-storey… that one over there… when I saw a man, hiding under the stairs. He had a GUN!'

He shouts into his radio. 'Code nine zero! The multi-storey off Baldwin Street!'

'Shall I show you where he was?'

'You stay right here!' He sprints off, and disappears round the corner. I take a quick glance around, and hit the remote. The doors hiss open, we dash through, and I close them quickly.

'I can't see a thing!'

'This way.' My hands feeling along the damp stone, I move forwards through the cave, straining to see in the half-light.

Becks' voice bounces off the cave walls. 'Where are we going?'

'Down.' I find the lift, but the door's closed, and there's no buttons for up or down or anywhere.

Becks runs her hands over the rock. 'Maybe it has some kind of sensor.' She leaps up and down on the stone floor, windmills whizzing around again. 'C'mon, Joe! Catch its attention!' So we do aerobics in this cave, and nothing happens. 'Maybe it's voice recognition.' She says, in a deep voice that's nothing like Monsieur's or Big Head's, 'OPEN!' Lift doesn't want any of it.

Then, I have an improbable idea. 'Perhaps it's French. OUVREZ!'

The door slides silently open, and we go in. In the dim light, we can see the button for sous-sol, the one for the ground floor, a black button and a red one with no labels. 'Pick a colour, Becks.'

'I don't do black.' The door closes behind us. We're going down. After maybe five seconds we stop, and walk out into a cave beneath the cave that's below the sous-sol. There's a wooden door in front of us, set into walls of solid rock. It looks centuries old; arched, like in a mediaeval building, with an iron knocker in the shape of a lion's snarling face. Becks' eyes sparkle in the shadows. 'Trick or treat?'

Clunk! The lift shuts behind us. Like it's not under my control at all, my hand reaches out for the lion's face. Before I can touch it, the door's opening.

'Come in quickly, both of you!'

We enter a luxurious cavern; expensive rugs, fine wood furniture, and paintings of Provence on the stone walls. No chandeliers this time, just wall-mounted lamps. Three doors open into other areas, looks like bedroom suites, bathroom, kitchen. There's another door, at the far end.

Monsieur waves us over to a sofa, opposite a desk with a PC on it that's squawking about an email that's arrived. He looks as cool as ever in the Armani suit, silver hair gleaming in the lamplight. But there's no half-smile this time. 'You are both risking your lives coming here. You have less than one minute to tell me why.'

He sits down at the desk, so we sit on the sofa. I don't know what to say. My brain's going, 'Fifty-eight, fifty-seven… ,' all over again.

Monsieur's grey eyes look at me steadily. 'You have a right to know who you have really been working for since you joined L'Étoile Fine Wines, Joe. Is that what is in your mind?'

I nod. Forty three, forty two…

His voice sounds as grave as it did that night in the carpark, when he showed me the bullet hole in the Bentley. 'It is some years since I gave orders of any significance in this organisation, Joe. It was not my decision to hire you as my chauffeur. And not my instructions that have put your life in such terrible danger, on two occasions.'

'Bertolini?'

WHUMP! The explosion sounds like it's just over our heads. Becks and I jump a mile high, but Monsieur doesn't move a muscle. 'It is time for you to leave, my friends.'

'What... what's happening?'

'There is no time to explain, Mademoiselle. You must go, now.'

WHUMP! The walls seem to shudder, and the lights flicker. One of the pictures of Provence crashes onto the stone floor, a small stream of rocky dust flowing out of the wall where it was hanging.

'Aren't you going to get out of here too, Monsieur?'

'I intend to leave, but only once you have both departed.'

Far above us, there's a quiet rumbling beginning, like a volcano starting to ooze trickles of molten lava before it goes up. Monsieur walks calmly to the door, and opens it for us. He takes Becks' hand. 'Aurevoir, Mademoiselle.'

'Aurevoir, Monsieur.' Becks shakes his hand, green eyes connecting briefly with his grey ones. 'Take care!' She moves out of the door towards the lift.

He grasps my hand with those long fingers, in a firm shake. 'Aurevoir, Joe. Tu as été un chauffeur magnifique pour moi.' Then his arms go round me in an embrace, like I'm a long-lost son. 'I owe you my life, Joe.'

I can understand the French. But I have no idea about the English. All I can do is stammer out the question I've wanted to ask him for so long. 'Monsieur... do you know my father?'

A grey cloud of dust floats between me and Monsieur as he releases me. 'Your father is Commander Julius Grayling, isn't he?'

'Yes. Were you friends?'

Even through the growing thunder above, I can hear his sadness. 'Once, I worked with your father, Joe. But then everything changed. And now, you two must save your precious young lives.' His voice is urgent. 'Go!' He pushes me towards the door.

Becks grabs my hand. 'C'mon, Joe!'

WHUMP! The ground shakes, and a shower of gravelly dust rains down onto the stone floor in front of the lift. Becks says sternly to the lift, 'Ouvrez!' The door slides open. Monsieur is watching us, willing us to leave. I'm glued to the spot.

'Come ON, Joe!' Becks drags me into the lift.

'We can't just…'

She whispers, 'We're not! But it has to look like it!' As the door slides shut, she looks around, up and down.

WHUMP! The lift shudders. Number four. 'God, I hate loud noises! There has to be a camera somewhere – otherwise how come Monsieur was expecting us?'

'Can't see one in here. Must've been outside the door somewhere.'

'He has to be certain that we've gone, otherwise he won't leave.'

'So – how long do we give it?'

Becks doesn't answer. She's staring at the tiny curls of smoke creeping in under the lift door. 'Ouvrez!'

We approach the snarling lion cautiously. 'It's bound to be locked. What do we do then?' But the door swings slowly open with just a push, and we go back into Monsieur's underground home. There's no sign of him. The rumbling overhead is slowly getting louder. The air is vibrating around us. Another picture smashes onto the floor.

'He's left the computer on.' Becks clicks on the mouse to bring up the file directory. There are hundreds of them, all with names in some kind of code.

'It's like the Bentley fusebox.'

'What?'

'Nothing.' I see a memory stick lying on the desk, and plug it in. 'There's got to be something here that can put Big Head away.'

'We haven't time to look at each one.' Trails of smoke are wandering lazily in through the open door. Becks rushes over and bangs it shut.

'We'll just have to copy the whole lot.'

'Here, let me. I do the fastest mouse in the West, pardner!' She starts clicking and saving so quickly, her hand's a blur. Now, we can hear the rumbling turning into a roaring. There's a groaning above us, like steel beams bending and buckling in molten heat. A sound like a gun shot, then another.

I glance around, half-expecting to see Big Head's bulky, dark-suited figure suddenly loom up behind us. 'I guess it's Bertolini who's behind the Big Bangs.'

Double-click, right click. Becks opens another directory. 'Shooters must've got boring. Not loud enough.'

'I reckon it's the only way he can destroy the evidence – there's masses of cocaine in the lower car park.'

I can't see what's left of the pictures of Provence that clearly. There's a haze between them and us. Becks wrinkles her nose as she clicks. 'Passive smoking – yuk!'

Now, we can hear unearthly shrieks of tearing metal. Thundering crashes of falling masonry shake the rock ceiling. One of the lights flickers again, and goes out. The roaring is all around us.

'How many to go?'

'Don't! It's like 'Are we nearly there, yet?''

'Sorry.'

Double-click, right click. BANG! My mind can see blue-glass fireworks soaring into the sky, and hissing as they shower into the docks, sending up geysers of steam.

'I don't think it was just the white stuff that Big Head wanted to send up in smoke… do you?'

I have to raise my voice above the roaring. 'But Monsieur seemed to know what was…'

'I can't copy this one – it's protected.'

'Leave it.' The haze is becoming a fog. My throat is dry and itching. Click, double-click.

Becks pushes a strand of red hair behind her ear, mouse hand slowing a bit. 'I think that when you dodged that last bullet and bumped into his fancy Jag, you messed up Bertolini big time.'

'You think he had another bullet… lined up for Monsieur… ?'

Smoke's billowing in now. The room's filling up with it. The roaring is deafening. 'We've got to go, Becks!'

'Just a few more…'

Another wall lamp flickers and dies. While I can still see, I look around quickly. Go through the drawers of the desk. Stumble into the kitchen and rip open cupboards, more drawers. There it is! I push the switch. A bright beam lights my way back to the shadow that's Becks. 'We've GOT to go, Becks!'

She does a final click, yanks the memory stick out of the computer and hands it to me. I stuff it into my back pocket. The torch blazes through a fog of smoke, as we grope our way towards the wooden door. I talk to the lift. It doesn't want to know.

Becks tries. 'Ouvrez, you pig!'

'Don't annoy it.'

'It's annoying ME!'

'The fire must've messed it up. We'll have to try and get out the way Monsieur did.'

'Like where?'

'That door at the back of the cave… ?'

As we run through the choking air back into Monsieur's apartment, all the lights go out. The screaming of melting, twisting metal is ear-piercingly loud. More walls and girders crash down above us. Smoke swirls all around, trying to fill our lungs. We're both coughing now. 'Get down! Below the smoke!'

We drop onto hands and knees, and find some air. The torch picks out the arched shape of the door at the back of the cave, and I reach up for the iron latch. We crawl through, and push the door shut behind us.

The roaring is further away now, and we can breathe. We clamber to our feet. 'Ouch!' The roof's really low. Becks can stand, but I'm stooping. We watch the beam of the torch as I move it across the rock walls. Suddenly it's trying to shine into a blackness ahead of us. 'Looks like a tunnel!' I keep on moving the torch round the walls. It finds another blackness, six or seven yards to the left of the first one. 'Pick a tunnel, Becks.'

'Your turn.' Her voice doesn't sound as though we're in a cave. No echoes. Maybe it's because the roof is so low here.

'Monsieur used to talk about the slaves – how they marched them underground up to Blackboy Hill to be sold...'

'Great History lesson, Joe, but we're doing Survival GCSE now!'

'No, listen! We have to take the tunnel that goes upwards. From the docks to Blackboy Hill, it's a steady climb on the road. The slave trail must go upwards too.'

'That's miles! And upwards to what? Can we get out up there?'

'I don't know. But we have to take the one that goes up. I reckon it's the one on the right.'

'Suppose Monsieur knew a way that comes out near the docks? They had to bring the slaves in secretly, didn't they? I've just got this feeling that the shortest get-out could be the tunnel on the left.'

'I thought it was my turn... ?'

The torch lights the rock walls as we grope our way into Becks' tunnel. It's so narrow that I have to go in front, scrambling over stones and boulders. The roaring above is distant now. There's just darkness, and the beam of the torch ahead of us, as we stumble along. Then, the path goes down steeply. I trip, and drop the torch. Becks grabs it. A huge pile of fallen boulders is completely blocking our way.

'Oh, poo!'

Now we hear the rumbling, getting louder. The tunnel's shaking. Small rocks are starting to fall, followed by larger ones, in front and behind. Stones bounce off our heads, as we race back towards the tunnel entrance. I can hear a creaking up ahead that I don't understand. Like something trying to tear itself away.

'Becks, STOP!'

'Why... ?'

I grab her arm and drag her backwards, as a huge shape crashes down just in front of us. 'Give me the torch!' More stones and rubble rain down, as I shine the beam on the monster in our path. 'I think we can just about get round it. Go on!'

She pushes herself between the giant boulder and the tunnel wall. 'Damn, I've ripped my best top...'

I follow her into the gap, feeling my chest being squeezed so tight I can hardly breathe. The tunnel floor shakes with another massive crash behind me, and dust pours onto my head and down my neck. Then I can't go any further.

'I'm through, Joe! Come on!'

'Can't...'

'Give me your hand!' Her hand reaches into the torchlight and grabs my wrist.

'You're pulling my arm off!' The tunnel wall scrapes my face, as I almost pop out on the other side of the boulder, and Becks topples over backwards. I drag her up, and we scramble wildly for the entrance, with more rocks thundering at our heels. Then we're out, gasping for breath.

The crashing of falling rocks goes on for at least another twenty seconds. The air is full of choking dust. Becks shines the torch on a wall of boulders where her tunnel used to be. We can hear the roaring above us again, and more gun shots, as blue-glass rockets into the sky. Smoke is mixing with the dust, as I croak, 'My tunnel, now?'

She brushes cave dust out of her hair. The coloured beads fly off into the dark. 'Only if it's got a power shower somewhere on the way.'

My tunnel isn't quite as low as Becks', but I have to stoop to walk. The ground is still so rough with stones that we keep stumbling. The air feels old, like no one's been in here for hundreds of years. Not much oxygen, but at least we can breathe again. The smoke hasn't got this far, yet.

She whispers, 'It's quite warm… I thought it would be all cold and damp.'

'Not as warm as it is in those posh offices now…'

As we scramble on, the roaring turns into a silence. There's just the sound of our feet, feeling their way over the rocky path. The clatter of a stone, as one of us trips up. It's then that I start to hear them. Tiny voices, echoing somewhere in the tunnel. I can't work out if it's in front or behind us. Or is it in my head? 'Joe… ! Joe… !' I stop dead.

Becks bumps into me. 'You alright?'

'I can hear…'

'What?'

'Can't you hear them?'

'Who? What can you hear?'

'Little kids' voices. They're like, calling my name?'

'I can't hear anything, Joe.' She grabs my hand. 'This place is doing your head in. Mine too.'

142

We stumble on through the blackness, with just the beam of the torch ahead. But I can still hear 'Joe... Joe!' Then I notice that my legs are working harder than they were just a few minutes ago. I turn to Becks' shadow behind me. 'The ground's starting to go upwards. Can you feel it?'

'Not sure. Could just be our legs getting tired.'

We trudge on, and I'm sure the ground's still going gradually upwards. It seems like hours, and endless miles, in the dark. And still these far-off little cave voices call me. 'Joe...'

I trip again, and fall flat on my face this time. Becks shines the torch down towards me, and I can hear her quick breathing. The light picks out a tiny human skull and tiny bones, curled up, beneath a ledge. My face feels the cool stones of the slave tunnel, as I just lie there and look at what's left of this little kid, who died so long ago in here.

Becks kneels beside me. In the torchlight, her fingers reach out and gently touch what was once a small hand. Her voice is quiet, trembling with anger. 'They took children... !'

As I clamber slowly to my feet, Monsieur's voice is in my head now. 'This place has a shameful past...'

We've been crouching, falling and staggering forever in this tunnel, when the torch picks out something that brings us to an abrupt halt. It looks like an immense, oily surface ahead, going on so far we can't see where it ends. We go a few more steps, and now I can stand upright. I take the torch from Becks and shine it upwards. It gleams on a high roof hung with hundreds of pale stalactites, some of them maybe sixty feet long, gleaming over this still and silent underground lake.

'Silly me, I forgot to bring the boat.'

'We'll have to lose the trainers. That's a pain.' We kick off our shoes.

'Give me the memory stick. I've got more layers on than you.' She jams it into her top. I stuff the torch into my back pocket, no idea if it's waterproof. Then I wade in for a few feet, and suddenly there's nothing beneath me.

I call to her through the darkness. 'I think it's very deep – but it's quite warm.'

There's a splash as she follows me. 'Eeugh! Smells mouldy!'

I have the feeling that we could be floating above an underground cavern that's as tall as a church. But Becks can handle herself in the water at least as well as I can. Our parents used to take it in turns to do the swim club run, although it must be a couple of years now since either of us has done any serious stuff. 'We need to have a plan, so we don't get separated.'

She spits out a mouthful of water. 'This is so disgusting!'

'Listen up, Becks! We do front crawl. I'll swim ahead. You grab my foot every four strokes so I know you're there?'

'You'll kick me in the teeth. Your feet are like propellers when you're doing front crawl!'

'Alright, you swim ahead and kick me in the teeth instead.'

'Deal.'

'But remember how to swim in a straight line, Becks. Otherwise…' I can feel her pitying look as she powers away from me into the dark. I follow, locking on to the wake of her kicking feet. One, two, three, FOUR, GRAB, telling her I'm there behind her.

We've been going for maybe twenty minutes when there's a colossal splash almost next to us. Something huge plummets past us into the depths. Becks stops. 'Don't tell me – Big Head's doing ballistic missiles now!'

'I… think it was one of those stalactites?'

'Must've been a one in a million chance for it to fall so close.'

'Or else it's the sounds we're making. You know, the way avalanches start?'

She whispers, 'Oh…'

I whisper back, 'Let's try not to kick above the surface.'

We used to swim up to three thousand metres in one go on a training night, but not with all our clothes on, like lead weights. I've no idea how long we've been going now. Feels like way more than the training run. It's a slower one, two, three, FOUR, when Becks' feet stop kicking and I come up alongside her. I can hear her hands splashing as she feels around, panting to get her breath back.

'It's solid rock. Just goes straight up.'

'And straight down? I'm going to take a look.' I take a deep breath and dive. The underwater rock face feels slimy beneath my searching hands. It just goes on and on, until my lungs are about to explode. My head bursts back up through the surface. 'Nothing.'

'My go.'

Becks' thrashing feet propel her beneath the water. And now, I feel like she must have done, waiting for me to come back up. After an age, she breaks surface, taking great gasps of breath. 'There's a hole, about ten feet below, maybe four feet diameter?'

We both tread water in the dark, thinking the same thing. Neither of us likes Underwater that much. And we have no way of knowing how much Underwater we've got to do. I breathe out slowly through my teeth. 'I can see why they closed these caves off. They're not exactly a tourist attraction.'

'Unless you really don't like tourists.'

We take a few minutes to fill our lungs with air.

'Ready?'

'Steady, go!' She dives. I'm close behind. I can feel her going straight down, close to the rock wall, then pushing herself into the hole. I grasp the rock at the entrance and shove my way after her, groping with hands and feet and all my brain, swimming blindly forwards like I'm on fire. Hitting my head on ledges I can't see. Hating everything I find that isn't the surface. I can feel Becks' kicking feet just ahead. Then I bash my head on another ledge and lose track of her completely.

My head's pounding, and my lungs are screaming for air now. And I think, 'We definitely could drown in here.' I read 'The Perfect Storm' once. Two ways of drowning. One: you lock up your windpipe so tight to keep the water out, you get no more oxygen. Two: you breathe in water, so you get no more oxygen. I can't quite make up my mind, when I crash into a ledge so hard it makes my head spin, and rocket up through the surface.

Taking huge breaths of cave air, I struggle to my feet, feeling sharp stones digging into them. I wade out of the water, pulling the torch out of my pocket. 'Becks?'

The beam cuts through the blackness – amazing, it's still working. It flashes around on a small, pebbly beach. Where there's no one but me.

—◇—

'Becks!' I turn the torch back towards the dark water. Nothing, just small waves lapping at the stones. Then the beam picks out something floating near the shore.

'BECKS!' I run back in, water showering up either side of me. I'm definitely hearing things now. Someone's humming this Christmas carol, 'Silent night... mmm mmm...'

She's lying on her back in the water, looking like she's woken up in heaven. Humming to herself. She says in a dreamy voice, 'It's amazing isn't it, this breathing thing?'

I splash up to her. She stands up, shaking strands of soaking hair off her face.

'God, Becks, I thought...'

'So did I! Where WERE you?'

'I had to do a single-handed fight with this giant squid. Where were YOU?'

She shoves a wave at me with both hands, and I splash her back. No worries about noise now, the stalactite bombs are a long way behind us. We wade out of the lake and onto the stony shore. The torch shines on layers of rock, and on a wooden door, with a trail leading up to it made by many weary, bare feet, some of them so small.

Becks gazes down at the footprints. She says softly, 'How come they're still here after all this time?'

'No wind or tides to take them away… ?' I walk round those footprints without touching them; I don't want my feet to smudge out even a part of their awful story. The door feels like concrete as I give it a shove. 'It must be nailed across from the other side.'

'Can you hear anything? Like cars, buses?'

'Nothing. Maybe there's just more tunnel…'

'Give me the torch.' Becks goes looking round, and comes back with a rock. She smashes it into the door, time after time. It doesn't budge. Breathing hard, she hands the rock to me.

I throw myself and the rock at the door like it's Big Head and I want to see him in small pieces. BASH! BASH! Splinters of wood fly into my face, but there's just more wood beyond. 'It's no good…'

'I don't suppose it speaks French?'

'Scream and shout, Becks!'

We both yell at max volume, 'HELP! HELP! SOMEONE!'

No one hears. I sit down with a bump, feeling like I did when the cops caught me driving underage, trying to find my dad. Becks sits down beside me. 'I'm so tired… can't stop my eyes closing.'

'DON'T!' I get up, every bone in my body creaking, sodden jeans clinging to my legs, and stumble over to the rock wall, shining the torch up, down, anywhere.

Then… 'Becks – over here!'

No answer. I go back to her. She's sound asleep, curled up on the pebbles. I shake her shoulders. 'Becks! You've GOT to wake up!'

'What…? Go away!'

'I think I've found something – come ON!' I drag her to her feet. As we approach, the Something looks like a small pool of shadow in the rock face.

'It's just a hole.'

'No, look. It's more than a hole. It's going into the rocks.'

'Could be only a few yards.'

'Yes – or it could be our get-out, Becks. What've we got to lose?' I squeeze myself inside, head and shoulders, then the rest of me, and shine the torch ahead. 'It's going upwards!'

'I'm here, don't kick my face!'

We're like worms, wriggling slowly forwards inside the hole. It feels horrible because we could get jammed in it and not be able to go on or go back. I didn't mind the tunnel so much because at least we could move around. But here in this narrow chimney, I can hear my heart banging in my ears. The torch beam waves around in total blackness. Harsh rock scrapes the skin off my hands as I drag myself upwards. 'You still there, Becks?'

'If you could just kick less stuff in my eyes… ?'

'Do you think some of those poor slaves tried to escape this way?'

'If I'd been them, I'd have tried it.'

The rock is crushing my ribs now, like the boulder was. I'm starting to panic in this choking darkness.

My chest is closing in on me. My bare feet scrabble at the rocks as I try to keep shining the torch. 'You OK, Becks?'

I've never heard her sound so tired. 'I'm thinking chocolate – it helps. Think chocolate, Joe.'

I'm not sure if I can squeeze through this next bit. It's so tight, I'm terrified of getting stuck. Not sure if I could go backwards, either. I think chocolate, and move another six inches upwards.

'You OK, Joe?'

'Chocolate's good.' My arms and legs are so heavy. It's all I can do to keep shoving myself through this gullet that's trying to squeeze me to death. The climb's getting steeper now, and the rocks are slippery. At least that makes it a bit easier to force my way through them.

Suddenly, it's really steep. My foot slips. 'HELL!' I reach out my hand to clutch at something, anything, and the torch goes rattling away from me, flashing its light. 'Get it, Becks!'

'Damn… !'

Everything is black.

'Can you feel around for it? It could be wedged somewhere.'

'I can't see any light. It's gone, Joe.'

'We picked a great time to reduce our carbon footprint!'

She says thoughtfully, 'I s'pose we could die in here?'

'Nah, there's got to be a better place. C'mon.' I feel around with my hands to try and find a rock to grab.

Her voice is very small below me. 'D'you really think we'll get out, Joe?'

'I don't know. But what's the point in not trying when we might just make it? I mean, we might find out after we're dead that we could've made it after all?'

'Hmm.' Her voice sounds brighter. 'It must be amazing, or really annoying, what hindsight you have when you're dead. Or is it foresight… ?'

We don't talk after that. We haven't got the energy. It's like the weight of the entire earth is pressing down on us, wanting us to stop right there. But we don't stop.

We've been wriggling upwards for maybe another hour, when I get a feeling that it's not just solid darkness I'm staring at. I don't say anything to Becks, not yet. It would be too cruel if it's just me seeing things. Like I was hearing things with those poor little slave voices. But I keep glancing up, and each time, it's still there. I can't tell if it's right in front of my face, or high up in the hole. Or beyond the hole? I want to reach out a hand to try and touch it. This tiny piece of light, so small that I daren't let myself believe what it just might be.

A sudden clatter of rocks below me. 'JOE… !'

I slither back down to her. 'Grab my hand!'

'Where are you?' More rocks bounce away down the chimney. I slide further down, feeling wildly around for her. Find her hand, grab it hard and brace myself against the slippery walls. I can hear her feet scrabbling around, trying to get a grip.

'Hang ON, Becks!'

'God I HATE this place!'

I glance up. It's still there. And it's twinkling. 'Becks! LOOK UP!'

'What?… Ooh…' Comes out like a sigh. Her feet stop scrabbling. She's found a foothold. Her panicky breathing is slowing. 'Is it… ?'

'I'm sure it's a star.'

'No, idiot! I mean is it planet Venus or a real star?'

'Neither! It's just the disco they run in this hole every night for lost souls like you and me! Now COME ON UP!'

The air gradually starts to feel different. Smells fresher, not like this ancient dust we've been breathing. Then, I think I can hear the low hum of traffic, a long way off. That tiny piece of twinkling light is turning into one big star in the sky. It's shining steadily, pulling us upwards out of the dark.

Suddenly, I can see millions of street lights in the distance. My hands are waving around in nothing at all. 'This is our stop, Becks.'

She clambers up beside me. Gazes out over the far reaches of the sparkling city of Bristol, then back up at the sky. Murmurs contentedly, 'Definitely… planet Venus… the morn…' She flops down.

I can't keep my eyes open any longer. We must have fallen asleep before our heads touched the stone of that ledge.

CHAPTER 13

Light

'Joe… Joe!'

I reach out to stop Becks falling into the dark.

'Don't move, Joe, or we'll be flying with the seagulls!'

I open my eyes. Planet Venus's brightness is being eclipsed by a sky that's glowing gold and blue on the horizon. A breeze strokes my outstretched hand. I open my fingers to get more of it.

'Have you noticed where we are?'

'The top sightseeing spot in Bristol?'

The Bristol suspension bridge is only a hundred yards to our left. As the light spreads, it shines on the slim rods that hold this old bridge high above the river Avon. A few cars are moving slowly across it. Three hundred feet below, the tide's flooding in, nearly covering the muddy banks.

Birdsong is soaring into the sky from the woods on the other side of the gorge. The last time I heard birds singing before dawn, I was standing on that old bridge, on the run from a nightmare. Now, we've survived a far worse one, and I know why those birds are singing so loud. Who wouldn't want to sing when the light comes back?

'How are we going to get down from here?'

'We'll think of something…'

'You haven't got another pack of Revels on you by any chance?'

'We'll move into Thorntons for a week once we touch down.'

The ledge we're lying on feels like it's been here for millions of years. On our right, other cave mouths open out over the gorge. They must have seen pterodactyls swooping and squawking like the seagulls are now, as they cruise beneath us over the river. Then I take a closer look at where we are, and I can see something near me that's not a million years old. 'Look, Becks.'

'It's an empty Coke bottle, Joe. Not a rescue helicopter.'

'No one on the planet has an aim that could chuck it down here from the top of the gorge. So other people have got up to this ledge. Or down to it.'

'Well, could you give them a shout? I'll be late for school.'

'Ow!' A small shower of stones falls on my head. Then a bigger one. There's a slithering and scraping above us.

Becks ducks. 'If it's another… !'

'Yo, dudes! I've come to annoy you. You can run, but you can't hide!'

Sirens are wailing in the distance, as Jack waves cheerily down at us from the ledge twenty feet above our heads.

'Jack! What the hell are you… ?'

'Chill, big bro. They're sending a climbing team to get us all out – how cool is that?'

'But how did you… ?'

'It was nothing. Just brilliant intuition and reckless heroism that I'm far too modest to tell you about.'

'Jack, you wouldn't have any chocolate on you… ?'

A flash goes off to our left; I look back at the suspension bridge. It's filling up with police cars and camera crews. Another flash. 'Smile, Becks. They're taking your picture.'

'Oh-my-God, my hair!'

I can see Mum, frozen on the bridge, her eyes huge in her white face. Grandad's got his arm round her. Jack and I grin and wave to reassure them.

Mum just screams, 'DON'T MOVE!'

Another shower of small stones hits my head, and a voice calls from above, 'Stay exactly where you are!'

Someone else shouts, 'Get to him, it's going!'

CRACK! Dust rains down my neck. There's a rumble like an express train as Jack's ledge starts to tear itself away from the cliff face. It leans down towards me and Becks, like the ceiling's falling in. We scramble wildly backwards towards the hole. There's another massive CRACK, and this gigantic piece of rock tumbles slowly past us, blocking out the light, then crashes on down the cliff face.

Jack's legs are just above us, waving around in thin air above the river. 'Hey, Spiderman returns! Awesome!' He's roped on with a harness, a climber beside him reeling off instructions. We watch, as Jack braces his legs against the rock, and gets pulled quickly upwards. 'See you at the top, dudes!' In seconds, his feet are out of sight.

More flashes from the suspension bridge. A reporter sounds like he's doing a live broadcast. 'The boy's around fifty feet from the top now. It's incredible. He's laughing and chatting to his rescuer as though he's actually enjoying this!'

'Your go, Becks.' My mouth is feeling drier than it's been for the whole of our underground journey.

Two legs come into view as Spiderman 2 swings down next to her. 'Done any climbing before?'

'Not till last night.'

'I'm going to pass you this… put it on slowly, and clip it at the front.'

'It's not exactly Versace…'

'The next big thing when they see you on TV in it, Becks.'

'Not on my worst ever bad hair day!'

The climber grins. He's about twenty, with a tanned, outdoor look. 'When the rope goes taut, go with it. You'll swing out at first, but don't worry, I'll steer you into the cliff face. Lift your feet like you're going to stand on it, then push out to let the team pull you up.'

'No chance of a lift in a helicopter then?'

'Trust me – this is way safer than a helicopter rescue!'

Her green eyes look at me quickly.

'Think chocolate, Becks!'

She gives a small squeal as the rope pulls her up and off the ledge. I watch her, my stomach tightening, as she swings slowly around over that yawning drop, the river like a silver ribbon, so far below. Her voice is squeaky as she yells, 'Remind me never to do a parachute jump for charity!' Then Spiderman 2 grabs the rope.

On the bridge, Anchorman is in full flow. 'The girl's got her feet on the cliff face now, her expert climber coaching her every inch of the way. She's getting the knack, long red hair billowing behind her in the breeze. And it's a breeze that seems to be getting stronger now. We can feel it up here alright! Over to our weather studio. Rachel! Are the conditions about to take a turn for the worse?'

I wish I could switch him off. I wish I could switch everything off. I hate heights, even more than Becks does. And I haven't got her guts. I can do lying here and admiring the view. But as for moving one concrete leg to get off this ledge…

Stones fly past as feet bounce down the cliff face towards me. Then, a face I've seen before is right in front of mine. Robocop Dave grins cheerfully. 'Not you again! Haven't you got a home?'

'I didn't know you do climbing in the police.'

'I rock climb for fun. But when I heard who was hanging off the cliff I thought I'd drop by and say hello.' He passes me the harness, I clip it on, and he waves towards the cliff top. 'Go!'

The rope goes taut and drags me off the ledge. I'm swung out over the river, my legs flailing around in nothingness. Then I feel his hand on the rope, guiding me onto the cliff face. 'Just relax – the guys up there won't drop you, mate.'

I plant my feet, muscles protesting, brace my legs like I saw Jack and Becks do, and push. A strong tug whisks me upwards before my feet hit the rock face again. Once more, I force my legs to bounce me outwards over the river, and I don't look down this time. Another powerful tug carries me on up the cliff.

'Nice one, Joe. Not that far now.'

Anchorman could have a coronary if he doesn't calm down. 'The last climb out of certain death! Despite the wind that our weather studio is telling us will increase to four knots soon – what's that in miles per hour, Rachel?… Anyway, it's going magnificently well! And thankfully, no sign yet of the gales that could tear these brave young men off the cliff face and into infinity. Now they're only around twenty feet from the top of the Downs. So near, and yet SO far! The young man is talking with his climber, and our reporters tell me that he's the brother of the daredevil who was chatting so casually with his rescuer only ten LONG minutes ago. WHAT a scene, only the morning after the explosions that tore the city centre apart!'

As we get to the edge of the cliff, hands shoot out from all directions, grab me and pull me onto the grass. Dave grasps my hand. 'Well done, mate. The boss'll be over shortly.'

'Thanks, Dave.'

There's an eruption of applause from the crowd on the bridge. People are cheering and waving, and a dude throws his woolly hat in the air. The wind gusts it straight into the river. Now the cameras are filming this as well, and Anchorman's telling everyone all about it.

It's a weird kind of picnic on top of the Downs. Jack's glugging a flask of tea – or something. He passes it to me. 'This stuff's amazing – try it!' I take a mouthful. It's hot, and sweet… and it's tea.

Becks is taking huge bites from a bar of Dairy Milk, as though it's going to disappear into thin air any second. She passes me another one, mumbling, 'First aid is chocolate!'

Mum and Grandad are hugging everyone, not just Becks and Jack and me. They hug the climbers, the ambulance crew, even DI Wellington. He looks like he's used to this sort of thing.

I'm about to say to Mum, 'Sorry...', for the four hundredth time, when DIW comes over to me. He shakes my hand, and claps me on the shoulders. 'You had us a bit worried there, Joe, when we couldn't find you in those caves.'

'How did Jack find us?'

His radio blares, and he speaks into it brusquely, 'Just the usual press statement. The kids are safe and well. Any other questions, no comment!'

He turns back to me, his voice quieter, bushy eyebrows frowning, but not like he's angry. 'He's got extraordinary recall, your little brother. A quick mind, too. Up at the Blackboy Hill tunnel entrance, he remembered a dotted line on the map of the caves we'd been using. Guessed that it could be the hole you two climbed up through, and worked out that it had to come out near the suspension bridge. Went up there, saw you two sound asleep on that god-damn ledge, and called us.'

'Music memory.'

'Sorry?'

'Jack is an amazing musician as well as a really annoying little brother.'

'Inspector!' Becks comes over to us, wiping chocolate from her mouth, and holds out the memory stick. 'It's got a bit wet and dusty.'

He takes it slowly, staring at it. 'What's all this, then?'

'Most of the files from the computer in Monsieur's apartment, three floors below the office block.'

DIW's eyebrows are joined up now. 'I can see the pair of you have got quite a story to tell me.'

I add, 'You might find something you could use against Big Head… I mean, Bertolini…'

'And against the mysterious Monsieur?'

Becks and I exchange glances.

'We don't think the drugs were Monsieur's doing, Inspector.'

'What makes you so sure, Joe?'

'He told us, down in his cave room, just before the explosions started… Said he didn't give the orders, hadn't done for years.'

'What else did he say?'

'He said he owed me his life. As though, if I hadn't dodged Big Head's bullets, and you guys hadn't been on the case, there would have been one more, for him.'

'And?'

'Then he said we had to go.'

There's a slight smile on DIW's face that I don't much like. 'Your Monsieur, whatever his real name might be – and we have some ideas on that – is highly intelligent. I wouldn't have expected anything less from him.'

I'm starting to feel angry now, but I know I mustn't let it show. 'I really don't think he was lying, Inspector.'

'Maybe, maybe not. Now,' He starts to lead us towards one of the squad cars, 'it'll take at most ten minutes at the station before…'

Becks cuts in. 'He spoke in French!'

DIW stops dead. 'What?'

We're almost at the car, and now I can see the tall plume of black smoke coiling up into the sky from the docks.

'His accent was perfect, wasn't it, Joe?'

'I'm sure he's French, Inspector. I just couldn't believe it before, because his English was so good.'

DIW looks thunderous as he waves us into the car, and gets into the front passenger seat. Becks whispers, 'He doesn't want Monsieur to be French, does he?'

'I s'pose it doesn't fit with the other information he's got.'

'Wonder how much information he has on Monsieur?'

'One thing's for sure; he's not getting anything else out of us!'

To our relief DIW doesn't keep us long at the station. 'I'll need you both to come back in the day after tomorrow, and make a formal statement. Can you make it for three o'clock? I'll send a car at two thirty.'

I start to say, 'It's OK, we'll take the train', when Becks grabs my hand with a warning squeeze. 'That'll be fine, Inspector.'

As we walk towards Mum's Citroën, she hisses, 'One hint that we're not being super co-operative, and he could start to take an interest in us as well as Monsieur!'

Mum turns to us with a little smile as we squeeze into the back seat with Jack. 'Your grandad's got a surprise for you, Joe.'

Becks and I have had enough surprises for now, but I smile back. 'Cool.'

'Hey, Joe! The dude who took me up the cliff says he runs a climbing club, an' I can join. They go up the gorge all the time!'

To my relief, Grandad chips in: 'You can join when you're a little older, Jack. I don't want to watch my grandchildren hanging off cliffs again for a while, thanks!'

As we reach Stroud, Mum takes a different route from usual, and pulls up outside a garage. A guy in red overalls with a long pony tail comes out, wiping his hands on a rag. He grins at me. 'Mornin', Lewis!' He turns to Grandad.'Have to say, we're quite pleased with it.'

We follow him inside and I stare. 'This is my car?'

Grandad runs an appreciative hand along the new paintwork. Then he reaches inside, pulls the bonnet lever and inspects the engine bay. For a strange half-second, I wonder if it's him I've inherited my car craziness from. His voice is careful: 'Not bad.'

Becks opens the driver's door. 'Can't be your car, it smells really nice.'

Jack gets in. 'New carpets. You'll have to get busy with the Pot Noodles, Joe.'

I sit at the wheel. No smell of leather, no sat nav, no massive engine. And no white stuff in the boot, with cameras watching everything you do. No contest. The Bentley's pants to my Peugeot.

CHAPTER 14

Monsieur

'Shall I come down and collect you when it's over?' Mum makes it sound like I'm going on an operating table. It must be the sight of the police car waiting outside.

'No worries, Mum. We'll get the train.'

'You'd better have some money, then.' She rummages in her bag and passes me a twenty pound note. 'Will that cover it?'

'More than. Thanks, Mum.'

As the driver pulls away, I wave at her small figure standing forlornly at the gate, and I think, 'This is going to be absolutely the last time she has to look at me sitting in a cop car.'

When we get to Becks' house Steve's waiting with her on the pavement. He grins and gives me a thumbs-up. 'Good to see you back in the land of the living, mate. What's 'shooters' en français?'

'Shut up, Steve!' Becks kicks his ankle. He waves cheerfully, and goes back inside. Becks slips into the car beside me, her hair swishing around in a breeze of fresh-smelling shampoo. 'You look different. Let me guess…'

'The shower's different. Think I've blocked it.'

'Too much information!'

I keep my voice down as the car moves off. 'Talking of which – we need to be careful what we say to DIW.'

She whispers, 'D'you think he's going to give us a grilling?'

'Well, he's going to want a blow by blow account, isn't he?' I'm whispering too, now. I don't think this car has mics and cameras, but I'd rather not chance it. 'Problem is, he's obviously convinced that Monsieur's the boss.'

'Then we'd better unconvince him!'

'I'm not sure how easy that's going to be, Becks.'

She looks out of the window as the car takes us down the M5. In the fields on either side sheep are grazing peacefully in the sunshine. We pass Michael Wood services. In my mind, I can see the Bentley rocketing off the motorway and up the slip road, headlights blazing into the dark. Becks turns back to me, green eyes thoughtful. 'Monsieur didn't seem surprised by the explosions, did he?'

'That's point one that we don't share with DIW.'

'As if!'

'He must've known what Big Head was planning, but by then it was too late for him to do anything except get out.'

'He must have known quite a lot. Like, when it was going to start…'

'Point two that we keep to ourselves.'

The driver reaches up to adjust his rear view mirror; we go quiet and watch the traffic on the M32. As we head towards the city centre Becks leans sideways to pick up her bag, and whispers into my ear, 'Is there a point three?'

'And four. I've forgotten both of them!' I try to re-run the thoughts that were going through my head while I was in the shower, but all I can remember is Mum shouting, 'There's water coming through the kitchen ceiling!'

D I Wellington takes us into a room that's more like a police cell; bars at the window, no carpet on the concrete floor and just a table with three chairs. On the table there's a tape recorder that looks like it should be in a museum and a closed laptop with a grimy film on the lid.

Becks glances sideways at me, and I wince as Point 3 resuscitates itself and hisses in my ear. Of course – we should have gone over exactly what we said to DIW yesterday. I bet she's doing just what I am; racking her brains to remember. I feel as nervous now as I did on the side of that cliff.

'Thanks for coming in, you two. Don't be put off by the austerity of this place. It'll give us some peace and quiet away from the phone, to get this interview done and dusted as quickly as possible. Sit yourselves down.' He switches on the recorder.

It's all going fine till we revisit Big Bang Number One.

'How did Monsieur react to the first explosion?'

Neither of us speaks, then we both speak at once.

'He jumped a mile high, like we did.'

'He said both of us had to get out.'

'One at a time, please. Joe first.'

'He did jump a mile high, then he said we had to get out.'

DIW looks at Becks.

She doesn't blink. 'That's how I remember it, too.'

'How would you say he looked, Joe?'

'Really scared.' I remember Leah Wilks' nails tearing into the Bentley's leather seat. 'Like, his knuckles were white.'

'Very observant of you. And what was your impression, Rebecca?'

Becks hates being called that, but she doesn't even wrinkle her nose. 'He looked like he'd had the shock of his life, Inspector.'

He stares at us both, long and hard, for a few seconds that feel like hours. 'Why did you stay on in a burning building to copy those files? Joe?'

I feel a wash of relief; it's so much easier to tell the truth. 'We were hoping there'd be something that you could use to get Bertolini locked up.'

'You must have known that you were risking your lives.'

'Not at the time. We thought we could get out in the lift.'

'And then you found you couldn't?'

'No, it wasn't listening anymore.'

He frowns like I've made a cheap joke. Becks jumps in. 'The lift was voice-activated, Inspector. The smoke must have got into it.'

DIW shifts and leans forwards in his chair, looking straight at me. 'I'm going to ask you an important question, Joe, and I want you to think very carefully about your answer. Did Monsieur tell you to copy those files?'

'No way!'

'He was still your employer. It would have been a life-threatening – and illegal – order, but you might have felt compelled to obey it. You won't incriminate yourself, whatever your answer is. Provided it's the truth, of course.'

I look straight back at him. 'He didn't tell me to copy the files, Inspector. It was all my idea.'

'Then why do you think he left the computer running?'

I just knew DIW was leading up to this. It's Point 4, that I was thinking about before the shower flooded the kitchen. Why DID Monsieur leave the computer running? My brain crashes, and refuses to reboot.

Becks parachutes in again, green eyes blazing. 'It's obvious, isn't it? When the building started to explode, everything was going to go up in smoke not long after we'd all left. Monsieur didn't know we were planning to go back in there. He thought he'd made sure that we'd gone. And he didn't have long to save his own life. What was the POINT of wasting precious time shutting down a computer?'

Wow. Becks should be a lawyer; she'd earn zillions. Put like that it all makes perfect sense. DIW must think so, too. Click! He switches off the recorder, shaking his head slightly. 'Would either of you like a cup of tea?'

'We're OK thanks, Inspector.' Becks looks deliberately at her watch and then at the door.

But I'm not done yet. 'Are you getting some useful stuff from the memory stick?'

His voice is cautious. 'The boffins have made a start. They tell me that some of the files are difficult to get into…'

'Oh…'

'However, the indications are that there's information on that little stick that could help us seriously undermine a major international drugs cartel.'

'Right.'

He takes out the tape. 'But the fact remains that two of our big fish are still out there, fighting fit, and we want them on the barbecue. Until both of these men are in custody, you and your family could still be at risk. You too, Rebecca.'

A Becks foot starts to tap quietly on the concrete floor. He continues, 'I want you to be very careful. If someone you don't know tries to contact you, or if you see anything that gives you cause for concern, you must let me know straightaway. Will you both promise to do that?'

We nod solemnly.

—m—

'I don't believe it! He still thinks Monsieur's a drugs warlord!'

'I think it's 'godfather'… or 'supremo'?'

'Whatever!' Becks shakes her red hair impatiently, as we walk past shops that are closing down for the night. 'What are we going to do about it?'

'What can we do? Look, we copied hundreds of files off that computer. There's got to be some stuff that points the finger at Big Head and takes the heat off Monsieur.'

The sun sinks slowly through trails of pink and gold clouds, as we wander along the docks. Becks keeps pushing her hair behind her ears. She's still fizzing with anger. I look at the low sun shining on the water and the swans cruising lazily around, feeling a rush of thankfulness for just being able to see sunlight again when I once thought we never would.

We get to the ruins of the blue-glass office block. No smoke is rising now. It's just a huge pile of twisted girders and rubble, maybe fifty feet high. No more leather sofas, luxury apartments and fine wines. Barriers fence off the site. Cranes, bulldozers and diggers are all lined up, ready to start work tomorrow. Becks stares at them, and I can see that another thought has started to bob around in her brain. 'In between those loud noises, did I hear you ask Monsieur if he knew your father?'

'Monsieur was in the photo of Dad that Mum gave me.'

'Why did you wait until the roof was falling in to ask him if he knew your dad?'

'It was only when we were in the cave room that I knew for sure I could trust Monsieur.'

'What did he say?'

'That he'd worked with Dad once... but everything had changed. He sounded very sad.'

'That was it?'

'Then you and I had an urgent appointment with the lift.'

We walk slowly on in the direction of the station. Becks takes a last glance back. 'Do you think Monsieur got out?'

'How will we ever know?'

'If he's caught and arrested?'

'He's too clever for that.'

'Then you do think he got out?'

'I hope so. If he did I know how he'll get away from the police.' I tell Becks all about Monsieur's yacht. 'He can sail back to France and no one can stop him. I bet that's what he does.'

Becks twirls a strand of hair thoughtfully. 'What if it was Monsieur who blew up the building?'

I stop dead and stare at her. 'Why would he nuke his own offices?'

'He told us he wasn't the boss. So the boss must be Bertolini. Suppose he'd been forcing Monsieur to let him use the wines business as a cover for the drugs?'

'You mean, he had some kind of hold over Monsieur?'

'It's possible, isn't it? Maybe something in Monsieur's past… like, Bertolini was blackmailing him?'

'So… what changed?'

'Us getting the police onto Bertolini?'

'If Monsieur laid the explosives, it would explain why he told us to get out. And why he wasn't surprised at the Big Bangs. But he lost everything…'

Becks says quietly, 'He must have hated Bertolini, to let it all go like that.'

My brain's going faster than it was ever designed to. 'But, what kind of hold could Bertolini have had over Monsieur?'

'Whatever it is, he could still have it. The police haven't caught him yet.'

'And he won't be too happy about what Monsieur's done to him. In fact… if he knows that we tried to help…'

'Bertolini will be after us all now, won't he? Like he came after you?'

Organisations like this never forget. They're a kind of Mafia.

'I s'pose that's why DIW told us to be careful. But boss man must have other things on his mind, with the police on his back.'

Becks shoves the strand of hair behind her ear. 'I wouldn't be too sure about that. He pulled out all the stops to give you a job to die for, didn't he? C'mon, we'd better go for the train.'

I owe you my life, Joe.

I don't move. 'If Monsieur laid the explosives, why was he still there when we arrived?'

'Unfinished business? He was on the computer, emailing maybe? He must have known how to get out so the police wouldn't see him.'

'So, why did he say he owed me his life?'

'Because of the bullet Bertolini had lined up for him – that's what we thought, wasn't it?' Becks turns to me, frowning. 'No, you're right. It doesn't compute if Monsieur did the blowing up.'

I wish my brain would slow down, but it won't. 'I don't think he was going to leave, Becks.'

Her voice is quiet with shock. 'He was… why would he?'

'Because of this hold that Bertolini has? Maybe nothing mattered anymore, except putting an end to the drugs.'

'And then… we turned up. And he changed his mind – why?'

I gaze at the bombed-out office, seeing me and Monsieur hurtling round the test track in the mighty Bentley. 'I've got to talk to him, Becks. He's the only person on the planet who could maybe help me find Dad.'